Coming To

A Midwestern Tale

A NOVEL

CAREN UMBARGER

To Lynn,
Keep Coming To!
♡ Caren Umbarger

COMING TO. Copyright © 2011 by Caren S. Umbarger.

Requests for permission should be emailed to the author.
Visit her website at http://umbart.com

This is a work of fiction. The events and characters described are imaginary.
It is not intended that any reader should infer that these characters, actions
and locations are real or that the events depicted actually happened.

ISBN-13: 978-1463786021
ISBN-10: 1463786026

LCCN: 2011914045

Book Design by Paul Umbarger

Printed by CreateSpace
Charleston, South Carolina

For our grandmothers

Life is either a daring adventure or nothing.

HELEN KELLER

Coming To

1

Lillian slipped out the back door, pulled her skirt under her thighs and sat down on the stoop in the last, weak sunbeam of the day. In the stillness of the late October afternoon, a chill hung in the air. She wrapped her sweater tightly around herself. The old maple in the lot behind her house had delicately dropped all of its leaves into a pristine circle on the ground beneath it and Lillian loved that.

She took a big drag on her cigarette then shook the Globe Gazette open to the front page. All week long, the newspaper's headlines had been huge and black, the boldest she had seen since the war. And, bad news: **STOCK MARKET CRASH... INVESTORS FEAR WORST... BANKS POISED TO FAIL.**

The headlines in her hands looked optimistic: **STOCK PRICES RALLY**. She didn't know much about the stock market because she had never paid much attention to the financial side of things. Before she was married three years ago, her father had looked after her finances. Now, Morris, her husband, took care of all of that. She had no money of her own, anyway – just what Morris gave her for her spending allowance. Lillian thought they had plenty of money, but this current Wall Street mess seemed pretty big. It appeared that the trouble was going to have an effect on everyone. Lillian read on down the page.

> Senator Brookhart, Republican, Iowa, predicted today that if the severe decline of stock prices in Wall Street continued, "banks all over the country" would go into bankruptcy.

She sucked hard on her cigarette then blew the smoke out in a fast cloud and watched as it swirled up and dissipated in the calm air. What would it mean for a bank to go bankrupt? It sounded ridiculous to Lillian – too far-fetched.

She peered in closer to the paper to get a good look at a small article near the bottom. A group of area businessmen made a motion before the city council meeting that was held on Wednesday evening to boycott Jewish owned businesses in Mason City. Their concern was the rapid growth of Jewish owned businesses in town and the spread of Jewish families into the area. Stanley Peterson, a spokesman for the men, cited the coincidental rise of the Jewish population in Mason City and the country in general with the simultaneous instability of the economy.

Lillian sat up and took a deep breath. What on earth were those people talking about? Who were those men? She'd met Stanley Peterson. He owned the other furniture store in town and obviously didn't care for the competition from Scharf and Son's, her father-in-law's business. But, to blame the Jews for the stock market? That was ludicrous and Lillian knew it.

Practically everyone she knew – her entire family who was scattered around Iowa and the Midwest, and most of her friends in Mason City – was Jewish. For fifteen years they had maintained a growing congregation of over one hundred and fifty people. Most of the Jewish men she knew were merchants or junk dealers. And, many of them had been brought to Mason City and sponsored by her father-in-law, Reuben Scharf. All they wanted in life was a better chance than their parents had in the old country; to have nice homes and good education for their children, to get along, and to create a benevolent milieu where they could practice their faith and go about their daily lives without any trouble. And, for the most part, that's how things were.

A noisy pair of gray squirrels raced down the trunk of a big oak tree that stood next to the garage and plunged into a pile of dead leaves. Lillian watched them turn somersaults and chase each other across the lot and up another tree.

She had faced no persecution, that she could remember, for being Jewish as she grew up in her small home town of Hampton, thirty miles from where she lived now. But, just last month, someone in Mason City had set a cross on fire

3

on Ben and Sonia Levinson's front yard after Muslims and Jews had clashed in Palestine and news of it had reached the distant Iowan outpost of twenty eight thousand souls where Lillian now sat on her back stoop. The whole thing made her sad. Why did people have to hate each other?

She closed the paper, folded it, and took a last look at the front page. There was going to be a radio broadcast at 8:30 that night by Julius Klein, assistant secretary of commerce, over a nationwide radio hookup of the Columbia Broadcasting company on business conditions in relation to the stock market. She might listen to that – see how much she could follow. Morris would want to, anyway.

Lillian heard his name reverberate in her mind. Morris, Morris, Morris… her *husband.* What had she gotten herself into? She turned several pages until she found the local section then squinted as she drew in off her cigarette. Lately, she could hardly believe she had really married Morris Scharf.

When she started college seven years ago, Lillian dreamed of a career on the stage. She was in every production in the theater department at Iowa City during her four years at the University and was lauded in the town Herald and back home in the Hampton Chronicle as a "gifted dramatic actress with a bold future ahead of her." By the time she graduated, she was ready and excited about her career.

Morris Scharf came along and inserted himself neatly into her life as though he had always belonged there. As there were so few eligible Jewish men in north Iowa, she convinced herself that his aloofness, his need to be in charge and his lackluster personal advances were not as bad as they seemed. His shortcomings endeared him to her and she eventually acquiesced to his constant entreaties to become his wife. She couldn't see any reason why being married to Morris Scharf should impinge on her plans to act.

Her mother, gone now almost two years, saw it differently. Tears came to Lillian's eyes as she remembered their conversation the night they sat together on the porch swing and pushed off gently with their feet.

"Lillie, dear. Are you in love with Morris?"

Her mother was usually right to the point.

Lillian didn't hesitate.

"Oh yes, mama. He's so handsome. I know he'll be a good provider."

"Handsome? Yes... but is that enough?"

Rosa looked directly at Lillian who squirmed around and tried to get comfortable.

"What, mama? Morris is going to be a dedicated husband. He always does all the right things."

Rosa looked at her beautiful daughter, all eagerness and energy. She fingered the arm of the swing then mindlessly ran her hand over the worn, curved edge, back and forth. She spoke slowly, chose her words carefully.

"Having someone you're attracted to is important, Lil. And having enough money is important, too, that's for sure. But, so is being happy. I want you to be happy."

"Why? Do you think I might not be happy with Morris?

He's going to be a good husband, I'm sure of it. Jewish men always make good husbands."

Rosa folded her arms and leaned her head back. A cynical humph escaped from her chest.

"I've no doubt that he will take good care of you, in a certain way. But, is his personality interesting enough for you? Can you have a thoughtful conversation with him?"

Lillian had the swing going full tilt. She pushed off violently with her toes each time it headed backwards. Her voice went up a few notches.

"What matters, mama, in a marriage is that he does his job, and his job is to provide for his family. You know there aren't that many available Jewish men around here, anyway. You certainly don't want me to marry that awful Elliot Weinstein. Oh God, that would be a fate worse than death."

They both laughed.

"No, my darling."

Rosa brushed the hair back off of Lillian's face.

"Your father and I want you to be happy, that's all. I have to say, though, that you seem to have a great deal more energy and... intelligence than your husband to be."

Lillian stopped the swing with her feet and turned to face her mother.

"Are you saying that I shouldn't get married? To Morris? Don't you know? He really is intelligent. He's just quiet... opposites attract."

Rosa looked lovingly into the deep, dark eyes of her daughter. She sighed.

"I just have a prickle about this. Marriage is

compromise, Lillian. The most important thing is that you have mutual respect. I hope he will be able to respect your wishes and desires as I know you will his. I just don't want you to have to compromise yourself right out of business."

Rosa looked off into the mild evening. Lillian noticed a small furrow between her eyebrows. A robin sang its last, lonely call of the day.

"I don't even know what you're talking about now, Mama. Why would you think that I would marry someone who wouldn't respect me? I know that Morris respects me. He shows it in everything that he does."

"He's courting you, Lillian. They always put on their best face."

Lillian sputtered and shouted in a loud whisper.

"I can't believe that you don't have any faith in my ability to pick a good husband. Did your mother say the same thing to you before you married your husband?"

The two women turned at the same moment to look at each other. Rosa's face wore concern, Lillian was contrite.

"I'm sorry, Mama."

Rosa put her arm around Lillian and pulled her close. Lillian laid her head down on her mother's shoulder. For a few minutes they just rocked. Finally, Lillian picked her head up and took a hold of her mother's hand.

"Mama. I'm going to marry Morris. I love him. This is my life and I'm going to do it. I'll be a good wife, you'll see. He won't have one thing to complain about."

"I'm certain of that, Lil." She nodded her head slowly up and down. "He's a lucky man."

"We'll be fine, mama. You don't have to worry at all."

"All right, my beauty, I won't, then."

They hugged for a long time. Lillian breathed in the delicious scents of her mother.

Lillian wiped her eyes and took a final draw on her cigarette – held it up in front of her and watched the end glow. It was more and more apparent that, despite what she thought about him in the beginning, the truth was, her mother was right. Morris really was *not* a nice man. He was a bully and a, well, a tyrant, if she could say it out loud, which she couldn't. No one else's husband demanded pot roast on Tuesdays, spaghetti on Wednesdays, meatloaf on Thursdays, and something specific for each night of the week, every single week, every single month and you'd better not go off the schedule or there'll be hell to pay.

Lillian pitched her cigarette down and ground the butt furiously with the toe of her shoe. He was so insistent. It was the way he told her things – so impatient, such harshness. She gave the newspaper a sharp snap and it stood up at attention for her, then she swiped a tear away with her finger.

If it were just the control over the meals, Lillian was pretty sure she could stand him. But, Morris had it in his head that he was the supreme commander in their marriage… about everything. He controlled all the money, he controlled their social life, he controlled where everything was in the house. He had the say about marital relations, especially about marital relations, and he even tried to control what she wore. She was tired of being taken completely for granted and being treated like she was his servant instead of his equal partner - the way a good marriage was intended to be.

She tried to tell him numerous times that they could have more between them; more intimacy and enjoyment together, more spontaneity – maybe even some fun. It was something she was certain of, but she had no way to convince him. Her attempts to communicate sincerely with him had been met with rebuke and scoldings. Morris knew his place and his place was at the head of his household and Lillian's place was below him, at his beck and call. He made the decisions. After three years, marriage to Morris was not what Lillian thought it would be like.

She set the paper on her lap, pulled a wadded-up hankie from her pocket, blew her nose and then wiped it. As she pushed it back into her apron pocket, she spotted a small headline. The Mason City Community Theater was holding tryouts for their winter play, The Wizard of Oz. Lillian's heart leapt. She'd read that play – she could do it. She hadn't been in a play since college, since before she married Morris and before she had Marcie, her fourteen month old. And, although Lillian loved her daughter deeply, fiercely, and although she honestly made a sincere effort to be a good wife, it was on the stage, acting before a rapt audience, where Lillian knew best who she was and what immense expanse of happiness life could grant her.

She looked out over the tops of the houses across the street at the sunset that was in full display. There were dark clouds piled up at the horizon and from around their bright edges, long rays escaped across the entire sky, like smiles from God... a good sign. She closed her eyes and a little prayer of hope puffed free from her breast.

The first tryouts for the play were to be held that evening, Thursday, October 24, 1929, at 6:30 p.m. in the fellowship room of the Methodist Church. She could get Clara to watch Marcie – that way it wouldn't be an imposition on Morris. She chewed a finger nail. The play was to be directed by Harold Winston, a former theater major at the University of Iowa. The call was for all parts. She didn't even have the playbook yet and the auditions were that night, only a couple of hours away.

She stood and brushed off the seat of her skirt. How to approach Morris so everything would go smoothly? How to get herself through the next two hours until the auditions?

Before she went in, Lillian took a deep breath in the cool damp air and looked out over the trees to the sunset where most of the light had died and roiling purple thunderheads made their way across the Iowa prairie directly toward her. A quick shudder rippled through her shoulders as she hurried inside.

2

If the news of the day was true – that the stock market was rallying – then Morris Scharf was going to be fine. Even if there were further plunges he didn't stand to lose his shirt like some of the other businessmen in town. Most of his and his brothers' investments were in real estate, not the stock market. The Scharf brothers owned more than a dozen rental properties in Mason City and five farms in the fertile lands surrounding it... Clear Lake, Nora Springs, Garner. If worse came to worst, they could raise rents.

And, they always had the store: Reuben Scharf and Sons Furniture Store. Every fiber of Morris' being belonged to the store. It's what his thoughts were dedicated to, what his life was about. That, and the incontrovertible fact that he was born into the highest life form that a human on this earth could take: Jewish male. He would be fine as long as he had the store and his faith in the blessed Lord and gratefulness that he was a Jew and a man.

Morris pulled up to a stop sign, maneuvered the small latch then pushed the rectangular fly window open in the store car, a dark blue '27 Chevy. It was too chilly to have the big window down but he needed some fresh air.

Not one person had come into the store to buy today, not one. He had never seen it so dead. At lunch, the radio had called last Thursday's decline a fluke, and much of the selling of the last few days, the brokers in the interview felt, was induced by hysteria. The views of the brokers were that no one knew of anything disturbing to the general market situation. Oh yeah? Where were his customers today? All day long, a deep catch in his gut had aggravated his natural anxious tendency until, at closing time, Morris found himself delayed in the restroom while he ruminated over the looming economic downturn. A shadow of that discomfort remained as he drove home.

When he pulled into the driveway of his two year old house in the Forest Glade section of Mason City, Morris had his usual swell of pride. He had certainly done well for himself. He had built one of the nicest and largest homes in town in the newest and most desirable part. He was fully established in his father's furniture business. He was respected as a macher – a big shot – in his synagogue and the community at large and he had a terrifically good looking wife and a cute little daughter. Except for a son, what more could a man want?

The smell of meatloaf hit him the moment he walked in the side door. Good, everything was as it should be. He planned to listen to the assistant secretary of commerce on the radio after his dinner and perhaps spend a few minutes with Marcie on his lap before that, although lately she was more interested in her blocks than she was in him. He found Lillian in the kitchen at the stove as she mashed potatoes in a pot, her elbow high up for leverage. He was displeased that his meal wasn't waiting for him on the table and his voice showed disapproval.

"Dinner not ready yet?"

Lillian stopped her mashing and wiped the sheen of sweat off her forehead with her arm. *He couldn't even say hello?*

"Hello Morris. Yes, dinner's ready. Sit down, I'll serve you now."

As she heaped food onto his plate, she heard Clara and Marcie come down the stairs. They came into the kitchen just as she placed Morris' dinner in front of him in the dining room. Morris preferred to eat more formally with Lillian rather than endure the mess and interruptions of a toddler's meal time. Lillian accepted his wishes because she always had breakfast and lunch with her adorable daughter, and Clara was there to feed the baby her dinner.

How was she going to tell Morris about the play try-outs? She could just tell him plain and simple that she was going. But he'd flare up if she did - he'd be immediately angry. It was going to take some tact, even though she was certain that trying out for the play was the right thing for her to do.

She helped Clara find dinner for Marcie then fixed herself a plate, carried it into the dining room and sat down across the table from her husband who had been reading the paper but whose attention was now riveted on his fork. He tried repeatedly to balance his food so that he had an exactly equal amount of meatloaf and mashed potato on it before he would take a bite. The room was so quiet that Lillian heard his fork make little sounds as it clinked on the dinner china.

She couldn't eat. She had to say something.

"Morris?"

He looked up – interrupted, perturbed.

"Yes?"

"Um, how was everything at the store today?"

Morris sat up straight and looked at his wife, whose flushed cheeks and shining brown eyes enhanced her natural beauty. She *was* the best looking woman he'd ever seen. He decided right then that he would have her that night before he went to sleep. With that, he looked back down and continued his quest for the perfect bite.

Lillian tried again.

"Morris. I'm going out tonight."

When he looked up again with raised eyebrows she didn't wait for him to say anything.

"The community theater is having tryouts for a play tonight and I'm going to try out. It starts at 6:30, in a little less than an hour. Clara will watch Marcie and put her to bed."

She gnawed a spot on the inside of her cheek. Her heart pounded.

Morris set his fork down and pushed his chair back from the table an inch, sat up straight. His voice was humorless.

"Where?"

"The Methodist church over by the library."

"How late does this try-out go?"

"I don't know. I guess it should be done by 9:30 or 10:00."

Both sat in silence while he decided what to say about Lillian's announcement. She fidgeted with a loose thread on her apron and decided she'd wear her new tweed skirt and the lavender blouse with the bow. He sought an avenue in which to assert some authority. His position as head of the household required it.

"If you get a part in this play, what kind of commitment is this going to demand of you? You have a full time job here at home with your daughter and me to take care of. I don't want you running off to be in a play at night when you have family responsibilities. Besides, isn't that community theater run by goys?"

Lillian wasn't surprised by what he said because that was the kind of thing he always said. She had to think fast.

"Yes, it's mostly goyim. I think Marvin Schulman has something to do with it, too. I've seen his name in the paper. They're all good people, Morris. I'll..."

"I don't know how good any of them are. Someone vandalized the Levinson's last week, you know. What a mess... such a desecration."

He shook his head sadly.

"Every time something bad happens in the world, it's a Jew's fault."

Lillian reached over and put her hand on his.

"We know that's not true, Morris. Even though that's what some people think, it's not true."

He jabbed at the paper with his forefinger.

"Look at this! Peterson's trying to boycott us because we're Jewish – right here in Mason City! I don't want you associating with those people. They're all Jew haters."

This thing was way off track according to Lillian. She only had forty-five minutes to get herself to the Methodist church. This was not the time to tell him about her over-whelming personal need to be in the play.

"Morris, you and I both know that assimilation takes time – generations sometimes – and effort. If we want to continue to live peacefully with these people here in Mason City, we need to participate in the daily goings-on of the town. It would be good for me to be in this play. I can be a sort of 'ambassador of good will' for the Jews."

Her idea made some sense but he really didn't want her to do it. He liked her to be home in the evening. And the stock market – so unstable.

"Things are too unstable, Lillian. I say... not now. No. The answer is no."

She tightened her lips into a pucker, picked up her plate, carried it into the kitchen and set it on the counter. She'd skip dinner. Immediately, Marcie called to her mother.

"Mama, mama, mama…"

The baby waved a messy hand toward her and Lillian walked over to the breakfast nook where the high chair tray and a good deal of Marcie were covered with mashed potatoes and vestiges of meatloaf.

What could she say to him? What would do it?

She didn't want to get too close to her messy child so she kissed the top of her head. Clara Larson, her sitter, sat primly next to Marcie, her soft white hair done up in neat braids which circled her head. Clara, who saved her life on a daily basis and whose presence was so gratefully appreciated by Lillian, calmly fed the child a bite then spoke quietly.

"This would certainly be a good time for people to get busy with things they enjoy. This is going to be some hard times, I'm afraid. I'll bet lots of people in Mason City would like to go see a play... stop worrying for a few minutes about how bad everything is."

She picked up a cloth and wiped a blob off of Marcie's chin.

Lillian turned abruptly and returned to the dining room where Morris sat with an empty plate pushed aside, his nose deep in the paper. She stood beside him.

"Morris, listen. It's important for me to be in this play."

He looked up, startled. She caught his eyes and held them with hers.

"The play is the Wizard of Oz. It's a story about a girl who goes on a fantastical adventure just to find out that home is the best place to be. It's a play for our times, Morris."

She was on a roll.

"With things so unstable, as you say, in the country and all this trouble against the Jews, it's the perfect time to get the message of this play out to everyone."

Her voice rose.

"Besides, people will need something to do instead of listening to bad news all the time."

She needed to calm down.

Morris tried to think of something else to say to dissuade her. When he paused she knew she had him at a disadvantage… time to strike.

"You'll be proud of me, Morris. You know I'm a good actress and everyone in town will tell you how much they enjoyed the play and how I stood out."

Was this a good tack? She tried everything she could think of. It also occurred to her in the midst of her appeal that in a perfect world, she shouldn't actually need permission from her husband to do this. Begging was not out of the question.

"Morris. Please say yes. This is something I feel strongly about. I would like to make you proud."

It was not an unattractive idea to Morris. Maybe she could help some of the idiots in town see what kind of talent resided inherently in the Jews. He wasn't much for plays himself, he usually fell asleep, but obviously some people liked them.

"How often and for how long will this play require your services?"

She had him. Her arms circled his neck, her cheek warmed his briefly.

"Oh thank you, Morris. You'll see. It'll be wonderful."

He pried her arms away from his neck and straightened his tie.

"What is the schedule for this thing?"

Lillian was so excited she could hardly breathe.

"I'll know better after tonight and I'll let you know. Oh, thank you."

She kissed him again on the cheek.

After she ran up the stairs to get ready, Morris sat in the silent dining room, satisfied with his beneficence. When Lillian lit up like that, she was a sight to behold. And, she was all his. What a lucky man.

3

Lillian waltzed into the playroom hardly able to contain her glee – her audition was a half hour away. Marcie toddled up to her and Lillian squatted down, engulfed her in a swirl of Chanel No. 5 and her mother's crocheted shawl.

"Mmm, my little darling. You have a good time with Clara. She's going to put you to bed tonight and tomorrow we'll go for a walk in the buggy."

Marcie pointed toward the door and said "Ah-dah-ah" and Lillian chuckled. The child endured her mother's caresses then squirmed to get free to return to the blocks she had been building with.

Lillian and Clara went over the plan for the evening then

Lillian stopped off in the bathroom to check her face in the mirror before she went downstairs. Her cheeks were flushed and her eyes looked happy and eager. She liked her new bob even though it made her neck look absurdly long. The bow on her blouse wouldn't hang quite right so she retied it three times. She chose a dark red lipstick and applied it carefully, blotted her lips on a piece of toilet tissue and gave herself one last going over.

She imagined herself on the stage at the audition as the scarecrow, of all things. When she had read the play in college, she had envisioned him as a wobbly character, barely able to stand. Lillian leaned in closely to the mirror and, with her fingernail, scraped a clot of lipstick away from the corner of her mouth. Maybe she could try out for him. She knew she could do him exceedingly well. Her insides jittered.

Downstairs, Lillian found Morris in his chair in the living room engrossed in the paper while Amos and Andy played on the radio. As she walked over to him he looked up at her and, instantly, his eyes traveled down and up the full length of her.

"When will you be home?"

"When I'm finished; I shouldn't be much later than ten."

He looked back down at the paper and made a sound that was half way between a cleared throat and a harrumph. A loud burst of audience laughter interrupted from the radio. When Lillian leaned down to kiss him goodbye, he stiffened.

"What's that perfume you're wearing?"

She stood up. What was this, the inquisition?

"It's the same Chanel I always wear. Don't worry. I'll be home before you know it."

He'd agreed to it, but he didn't like it. For her sendoff, he ducked behind the paper and shooed her away briefly with one hand. But Lillian didn't see it. She was out the door.

She maneuvered her new, yellow '29 Cadillac roadster (that Morris had bought for her last summer) backwards down the driveway, put it in neutral, pulled the brake, got out, pulled the garage door down and got back in. As she drove away, a powerful anxiety overtook her so that, two blocks later, when she was about to pass by West Park, she turned in instead, parked under the light and got out. Down by the baseball diamond a couple of fellows horsed around with a ball and bat but they would have to quit soon – it was too dark out to play.

Lillian buttoned her coat and turned up the collar, lit a Chesterfield and leaned against the huge fender of her car. At that moment, a large black crow swooped down and landed a couple feet away from her in the circle of light afforded by the spot. It pecked at the ground once then looked up at her with a cocked head. When she kicked a foot to shoo it away, the bird merely stepped back out of her reach. From a nearby tree, another crow screeched its call and the big crow at her feet spread its wings, lifted off, and flapped upwards out of the light.

Lillian let out a huge sigh. It was a relief to be out of the house. She breathed in the damp, loamy smell of the creek that ran through the park. The air held a promise of rain and she remembered the storm clouds that had gathered at sunset. This was a good time to be in a play. The high holidays were over and winter was coming. She would have something to do during the interminably long, cold nights. That is, if she got a part, and she couldn't imagine that she wouldn't. What would Morris say, though, about her being gone to rehearsals three nights a week – for six weeks?

Just three years ago she was free to do whatever she wanted to at college. Now, her life was held tightly in check by Morris – by her wifely role. Too bad he didn't see himself the way she did. If one strand of his life was out of line, he couldn't stand it. He needed to control everything... everything. She dropped the butt; ground it out with her toe. Well, this play was something he couldn't control.

Just as the two men from the baseball diamond reached the parking area, Lillian hopped in her car and took off.

She drove east on 1st NW, over the tracks, past the new high school, where a few lights inside lit up the enormous windows. After she crossed Federal, Lillian turned right on Pennsylvania and pulled up in the dirt parking area of the Methodist Church next to an old Ford jalopy, then sat in the car for a few minutes and watched several people enter the side door. She had her usual pre-performance nerves – an undulating stomach and dry mouth. Would she ever outgrow that? Her watch said 6:28. There was nothing to do but go in.

She pulled off her driving gloves and hat then undid the buttons of her coat as she headed downstairs. At the bottom she hung it on a rack with the others'. The susurrus of people talking led her to the large Fireside room where Lillian stood in the doorway and surveyed the scene – about thirty people in all. She recognized a couple of women from town and nodded hello, but only one man looked familiar to her, so she walked over to where he sat – a small, wizened elf, behind a card table. Tufts of white fuzz sprang out on either side of the little man's head and lines and folds appeared in contours on his face when he smiled at Lillian.

"Well, hello there, Mrs. Scharf. Good to see you here tonight."

Lillian had to admit that it was nice to see a familiar face. It had been years since she'd auditioned for anything. Moody Luckle was one of the old timers who sang around town in the barbershop quartet, plus he was the next door neighbor of her in-laws.

"Hello Moody. How's Bertha feeling? Better, I hope."

"Yes ma'am. She's up and around again. Good thing, too. I was getting pretty tired of scrambled eggs."

He laughed heartily and several bystanders joined in.

Lillian got herself signed up for an audition. She was eleventh after Bessie Workman, whoever that was. Where had all these theater lovers come from? She had read newspaper accounts of the goings on for the past three years and had seen a couple of plays, but had never even considered acting again until a couple of hours ago. How quickly her life had changed direction.

With her playbook in hand, Lillian found a bench along the wall and studied the scene in Act One, Scene One where Dorothy and the scarecrow meet. It was only four

24

pages of lines. She read them over and over and imagined what she could do in her audition to grab the director's attention.

The director's attention, however, was already grabbed. Harold Winston leaned against a door frame across the room from Lillian and tried to maintain his cool demeanor as he watched her from afar. What a beauty. Just the way she carried herself, her ease with Moody and the others in the room, the intensity in her face. Such intelligent eyes. Who was she?

"Hey, Harold. Are you ready to start?"

It was Jane Romey, the tall, gaunt assistant director. Harold didn't ever want to stop his perusal of that woman across the room, but he had to.

"Sure, Janie. Let's get the ball rolling."

Just then, before Jane called the evening to order, Lillian looked up and, without prior intent, fixed her gaze directly on Harold. Their eyes met and locked. Lillian couldn't look away – she didn't want to. And Harold was a goner. Who was that woman?

Jane's deep voice boomed out over the noise.

"Welcome to the first night of auditions. We're going to use the classroom next to the Fireside room for our auditions tonight. You'll need to be ready outside the door while the person in front of you has their turn. First up: Bob Utne. Next in line: Cora Anderson. I'll let everyone know when you're due up, okay?"

The room burst into excited motion. Lillian pried her eyes away from the man's across the room and heard her own pulse pound in her head. What on earth? She stood lost amid the general confusion. From the look of things, he was the director, Harold Winston, and she was about to do an audition in front of him.

On a countertop next to the kitchen she spotted a water pitcher with some glasses and headed for them. As she began to pour, a hand reached out and steadied the glass for her. Lillian looked up into the wide, kindly face and multiple chins of Millie Blovak.

"Millie! What a nice surprise. I'm so glad to see you here."

"Well, it's mutual, my dear. I was wondering when you were going to venture into the Mason City theater world."

Millie's hair was greasy, gray and thin, shoulder length, and the fat on her arms and upper body struggled to be contained by her blouse. Lillian detected a slightly unpleasant body odor, but she didn't care one bit. She liked Millie. She knew her from Scharf and Sons' store where Millie did some design work for Morris.

Lillian drank half the glass of water before she could talk.

"I had no idea there would be so many people trying out. What are you doing here?"

"Costumes. I'm the costume lady for this one. But, enough of me. How are things with you, *Mrs.* Scharf? How's married life?"

She emphasized the Mrs. part. Millie was a single woman.

Lillian shot her a look. Could Millie see right into her; the way she said 'missus', as though she knew exactly what Lillian had been thinking earlier about Morris, about her marriage?

"Well..."

She tried to come up with a way to say it.

"I certainly have a nice home and a beautiful little daughter. You know that."

Millie turned and leaned her huge rear end against the counter, then folded her arms high up over her bosom. She didn't say anything, but she looked at Lillian with her eyebrows raised, and nodded. She waited.

Jane's voice reverberated in the room.

"Keith Sanderson, Kelly Canella, Mike Fletcher..."

Lillian wasn't sure what to say.

"I'm maybe not as happy as I was. And, nothing's really changed, either. At home, I mean. Morris is the same...."

Her voice trailed off as she remembered his reaction at dinner.

"What's wrong, honey. Can you talk about it?"

Lillian was mortified. Was she that easy to read?

"Listen, Millie. I can't talk about it right now. I'm about to audition for the scarecrow. By the way, what do you know about Harold Winston?"

Millie's face went soft, her eyes crinkled up.

"Now there's a sad story. He's such a nice fellow, too."

"Tell me more." Like a hunger in Lillian.

"I'd say Harold's a cautious man. His life's made him that way."

Lillian leaned in closer. She wanted to hear this. Millie went on.

"He's lived alone for eight years, since he was twenty-two. And he's borne the burden of his wife's mental incapacity completely alone for that whole time."

Lillian's heart lurched. She had heard only 'wife'. Well, what did she expect? She had a husband. What on earth was she thinking?

Jane's voice called out into the room.

"Hilda Joyce, Barbara Houser, Nat Kringlehoff."

Around them, people stood or sat and peered into their play books as they desperately tried to prepare for their auditions.

Lillian took a hold of Millie's arm.

"Did Harold tell you all of this? Tell me more, Millie. Please."

Millie nodded, and the two women huddled close.

"They met at the state declamatory contest in Iowa City when he was a senior in high school. Got married two years later, when she was eighteen and he was twenty. Henrietta Fry..."

Millie looked off – saw into the past.

"She was a wild girl from Clear Lake who loved all things theater, and who loved Harold Winston even more. She had a free spirit and no ambition, but plenty of talent and good looks, and lots of brains. They were perfect for each other. She had no real family, just a great aunt who had taken her in as a child and who died a few months after they were married. Then they had two good years together while Harold finished his theater degree in Iowa City and Henrietta kept house and acted in local plays."

She stopped – readjusted herself against the counter. Lillian was torn. Her audition was a few minutes away, but she had to hear the end of the story. In a split second, she dug in her purse for a cigarette and lit it.

"Go on, Millie, but talk fast. I'm almost up."

"Yes ma'am. He worked most nights as a janitor. But, right after she turned twenty, Henrietta changed. She began to drink every night – scotch – afternoons, too. Then, she accused Harold of improprieties with other women and despite his denials, she didn't believe him."

Lillian sucked on her cigarette until her cheeks went hollow then quickly blew the smoke off to one side.

"How do you know these things? Did he tell you all of this?"

"He did. We've worked on several plays together... we've grown into friends. He's a good man."

Both women looked up when someone shouted something at the top of the stairs, but the room remained relatively quiet. Lillian nudged Millie with her elbow.

"Keep going, Millie. Please."

"Where was I? Oh yes. She threw things and alternately wept and shrieked at him and demanded apologies for his imagined offenses. For Harold, there was no explanation for her behavior. When he tried to console her, she was belligerent. When he couldn't stand it any more and lost his temper, she huddled in a corner and cried."

The barge-like voice of Jane Romey cut in again.

"Mark Harmonson, Bessie Workman, Lillian Scharf."

Lillian fluttered her fingers to propel the story forward, but Millie was uneasy.

"Don't you have to go? They called your name."

"I'm okay... just keep talking."

"Okay. Poor Henrietta stopped taking care of herself and within a matter of weeks she looked like an old, worried woman: messy hair and dirty, wrinkled clothes. Harold was undone by his wife's transformation. He was close to finishing his senior year and had projects due... he was about to play Puck in A Midsummer Night's Dream. He tried to handle everything, but distress over her behavior forced him to confide in a doctor who immediately had Henrietta admitted to the hospital for observation. Between his night work, visits to his wife and his efforts to keep his own sanity intact, Harold found it impossible to keep up at the university. The day the doctors diagnosed her was the day he quit college... hopeless paranoid schizophrenic."

Lillian smashed her cigarette out in the ashtray on the counter.

"For kripes sake, Millie. That's a terrible story."

She scanned the room and took a few steps so she could see into the hall. A woman spoke her lines into the air as she waited at the door to the audition classroom. Millie folded her arms.

"Do you want to hear the end?"

Lillian whirled around, her eyes flashed.

"Can you finish it up fast? I've gotta go."

"Yes ma'am. After he had searched thoroughly and painfully in vain for an alternative, Harold had her placed in the hospital for the insane in Independence. The frail, oblivious woman he left with the nurse there bore no resemblance to the beautiful, lively Henrietta Fry he had married two years before. He moved back here to Mason City where his family lives, bought a small house with money he borrowed from his parents, and began to learn what it was like to let go of a person he loved when it wasn't what he really wanted to do. After a couple of years, she stopped recognizing him during his visits and he knew that she was never, ever going to be the girl he remembered. And Henrietta clearly didn't give one hoot about him any more."

"Lillian Scharf? Lillian Scharf?"

Jane sniffed her way through the room like a bloodhound.

"Is Lillian Scharf here?"

"Here I am."

She raised her hand and hugged Millie with the other arm.

"Thanks for the story. Wish me luck, Millie. Here I go."

"Break a leg, honey. You can do it."

4

Lillian entered the classroom silently while Harold, with head bent, sat at a child's desk and scratched notes with what sounded like a dull pencil. Two seats away sat a young woman with short, curly black hair who smiled at her and snagged Lillian's attention with her formidable buck teeth. She couldn't possibly be Dorothy, could she? Lillian had a moment of doubt about the whole thing, but decided to go on with it.

She knew that in order to have a successful audition she needed to suspend reality for a few minutes, which meant she had to forget that *that* was Harold Winston who sat in front of her. She spoke directly to the woman.

"I'm Lillian Scharf and I'm trying out for the scarecrow,

page ten."

At her voice, Harold's head popped up. He couldn't hold back the big smile that erupted on his face.

"Lillian. Hello, Lillian. I'm Harold Winston."

He sat for a moment and mooned at her then nodded his head sideways.

"And this is Sally."

Lillian gave him a cursory nod, but that was all. She ignored the butterfly convention in her stomach.

Sally rifled through to page ten, read for a few seconds, then spoke.

"Okay, go ahead."

Lillian closed her eyes, saw herself hung on a wooden stand in a cornfield, spread her arms out from her sides and let her head and her hands hang limp. One hand held her play book, from which she stole glimpses of her lines.

Harold Winston sat spellbound as the lovely woman in front of him, in her tweed skirt and lavender blouse with a bow at the neck, transformed herself into a male scarecrow – voice and all. He was particularly taken with her eyes. Not only were they big and brown, but their expressiveness floored him. Before she finished her first line he was convinced that that scarecrow didn't have a brain, but, ah, he had a heart. What a talent! Where had she been hiding? He darted a quick look at her left hand and was disappointed when he saw the gold wedding band. Hadn't she stared at him, too, though, earlier? Surely he didn't imagine it.

When Lillian finished her scene there was dead silence in the room. Sally's mouth hung open. For a few seconds no one moved until Lillian finally broke into a contagious smile that loosened the tension.

"Oh my," was all Harold said. He gazed at her like she was a priceless relic. A moment more and she would be distinctly uncomfortable.

"Um, thank you for the audition."

She did a little bow and fled the room.

Harold turned to Sally.

"Well, we have our scarecrow."

All Sally could do was nod.

In the Fireside room, Lillian was surprised by how many people had left already. She started to walk toward the counter but couldn't, due to severe trembling everywhere in her body, so she pulled around and backed up to the wall. The clock said 9:10. She did not want to go home yet for a couple of reasons, the main one of which was unfettered freedom – no Morris, and the usual weight of his presence – like night and day.

She headed toward the ladies' room. Why did she constantly think about Morris? What good could it possibly do? He wasn't about to change. If anything, he was getting more and more closed off.

When she opened the bathroom door, a small upholstered chair with a skirt beckoned to Lillian from the corner and she gladly sat. After a couple of deep breaths she found a cigarette in her purse and lit it up. Her audition went well. And, that Harold Winston… oh my, indeed. She'd never had such a visceral reaction to a man before. So attractive. She smiled and noticed her new bangs in her reflection in the mirror – raised her eyebrows a couple of times to ascertain whether they were straight or not. They were.

It was impossible for Lillian to perceive what she really looked like to other people, but she tried to see herself through others' eyes, nonetheless, every time she looked in a mirror. She stared into her own eyes, squinted, turned sideways for a moment to check her nose. It had a slight bump and a down turn at the end which she wasn't fond of. She stuck her tongue out and up and watched in the mirror until the tip of it just grazed the bottommost speck of her nose where it dipped down.

A sharp rap on the door… Lillian slipped her tongue back in her mouth. The bathroom door opened and Harold Winston stuck his head in.

"…closin' up…"

He stopped short when he saw Lillian seated in the corner. Their eyes met again.

"Uh, hello Lillian. I'm just… everyone's gone home. I'm glad I checked in here. You might've been locked in."

His eyes sparkled.

The tremble was back in her chest and it made it hard to get enough air. She stood up. His eyes were green. They bore into hers.

"You were wonderful tonight, Lillian. The part's yours if you want it."

She took a big drag on her cigarette, threw a hip out, vamp-like, and didn't miss a beat as she spoke in a broad southern drawl.

"Wah, Harold, ahm not the lay-east bit *an*-ter-es-ted."

Surely he knew how much she wanted the part.

Harold, not to be outdone, made a bow in the doorway and swept his arm in a flourish.

"Well, my dear," he looked her right in the eye, "*I* am."

Another shiver coursed through her... a double entendre. Lillian saw possibility gape before her. It was the wrong way to go – unquestionably wrong. But, she wanted that part in the play, badly, and his attractiveness had nothing to do with it. Well, maybe not nothing, exactly. She took another puff of her cigarette then crushed it out in the ashtray.

"I would love to be your scarecrow, Harold. Thank you."

He ushered her out of the smoky little room.

"You were far and away the best candidate for that part."

He helped her on with her coat, and as he lifted it up over her shoulders, his own arms wrapped around her to close it. Before she knew what to do, he buried his nose in the back of her neck and kissed her behind her ear.

"Mmm... you smell so good."

She turned around in his arms – faced him.

"Harold, I... I'm... I can't... I'm married."

It wasn't what she really wanted to say. She was surprised to find that she liked what was happening.

His anguished face was inches from hers.

"Forgive me, Lillian. I was out of line."

They stood close for long seconds. Lillian saw his eyes plead with her and, at the same moment, as a soft explosion went off in her heart, Millie's story came back to her.

"Millie Blovak told me a little about you. You don't seem so cautious to me."

Harold's eyebrows shot up.

"Cautious? Me? I guess that might be true."

He looked purposefully into her eyes.

"I can't help myself with you, Lillian. You're the loveliest woman I've ever seen... for a long time anyway."

Lillian allowed the warm bath of flattery to flow over her. He emanated sweetness, an attribute Morris certainly didn't possess. How pleasant it was to stand close to this unfamiliar man; safe.

"The call backs are tomorrow. Can you come?"

No hesitation.

"Yes."

He turned off the last hall light and they walked up the stairs together. At the top she stood with her back to the door.

"I'll see you tomorrow, Harold."

She fixed her hat, put on her gloves and gave him a little smile. Just before she stepped outside, he reached up and ran his thumb along her cheek. Her heart thumped.

"Tomorrow night, Harold."

"My God you're a beautiful woman."

"Tomorrow...."

She pushed the door open, ran to her car and leaped in. It was better not to look back. As she struggled to get the stick shift into reverse, the echo of Harold's kiss reverberated on the nape of her neck. She backed the big car around and felt, over and over again, his warm, shivery breath on her neck – his body close to hers.

5

Morris switched the dial off on the radio and sat back in his chair. Despite all the bad news, there was reason to be optimistic – stock prices rallied all day. And Klein, the Assistant Secretary of Commerce, sounded cautious, yes, but optimistic, too.

All this economic talk made him tired, and there was no break. Not even a baseball game to take his mind away. For Morris, the best thing in the world was to sit back in his chair with a cold scotch and soda, feet up, and listen to the announcer's voice... the slow, steady action of a baseball game – the crack of bat against ball – the cheers of the fans. Two weeks ago his team, the Chicago Cubs, lost the World Series in five games to Philadelphia. He could hardly stand to think about it. The Cubs had an eight run lead in Game Four, and were about to tie the series at two games, when the Athletics scored ten runs in the bottom of the seventh. After that, the Cubs lost their spirit and game five, three to two. It was awful for his team to have made it all the way to the series only to lose like that in the end. Now, he'd have to wait all winter for baseball to come around again. Good thing he had his Sunday morning basketball game with the fellas from shul.

He stood, walked over to the window and pushed the curtain back with the folded newspaper. Across the street, the Westley's dachshund ran crazy circles in their front yard under the gas light as Dick Westley stood on his porch and watched. When he noticed Morris at the window, he lifted a hand. Morris raised his paper and nodded, then stepped back and pulled the blind down.

Westley wasn't one of the trouble makers in town. From what Morris could tell, it was mainly Peterson and his cohorts who resented how well Scharf and Sons was doing and how well the hundred and fifty or so Jews in Mason City were doing in general. They worked as hard as any of the goys in town – no question about that. Why, a quarter of the businesses in the downtown were owned by Jews. Mason City would be a piddling little podunk without their presence here. Why did there always have to be one loudmouth like that fool in the city council meeting to stir up the ancient, dormant fear of *other* that rests in every man? Rests... and waits for its opportunity to rise up and have its say.

Morris checked his pocket watch: 9:30. What if today's

stock rally wasn't a true sign of things to come? What if the whole thing collapsed and everyone lost all their money? It happened to them in Russia during the revolution. How were people going to continue to purchase merchandise from Scharf and Sons if no one had any money?

A deep gurgle traveled downward noisily through his bowel and ended with a sharp cramp that doubled him over. He backed up quickly to the davenport and sat and rocked. Where was Lillian? He sent Clara home over an hour ago, after she put Marcie to sleep and washed the dishes. He read the entire paper. The only thing on the radio was classical music, which he pretended to enjoy around Lillian, but which secretly numbed him to the bone.

He needed something to settle his gut – like a drink from his precious bottle of Scotch, a protected commodity during this ridiculous prohibition. For his tender abdomen's sake, he walked stooped over to the cabinet by the dining room door and found his prize, poured himself a shot and downed it. As it burned its way down his chest, Morris saw the headlights from Lillian's car arc across the living room as she swung into the driveway. He positioned himself back in his chair with the paper up before him and heard Lillian open the back door and come in the house.

She set her purse on the credenza, pulled her gloves and hat off, unbuttoned her coat and hung it on a hanger in the closet. The faded, hours old smell of meatloaf hung in the air. Now she would see Morris. Lillian tucked away her happiness, which hadn't left her all the way home, ran her hands through her hair and walked into the kitchen where she took a glass out of the cupboard and let the water run.

From the living room came the rustle of a newspaper and inside her, an instant wobble of unease. She drank down the entire glass of water, then sighed. There was no way to avoid him. The thing was, she hadn't done anything wrong. If anybody had, it was Harold. The fact that she enjoyed it was a credit to her sensual nature, which she had forgotten she even had before tonight.

The newspaper rustled again, louder. Lillian walked in and stood next to the banister. He stayed behind the paper.

"Hello. I'm back."

She rested her arm on the smooth oak rail.

"Everything okay with Marcie?"

Morris folded the newspaper importantly on his lap. When he looked up, his eyes did a quick check down and up his wife. Her cheeks were rosy, her eyes shone.

"Marcie? Yes, fine."

He stared at her.

"Well. This play must be good for you. You look... radiant."

Lillian detected a slight sneer in the way he said radiant that she had never noticed him do before. She proceeded with caution – tamped down her excitement.

"It was a good night."

She clasped her hands.

"I did awfully well in my audition... I got the part. I'm the scarecrow. Rehearsals start tomorrow."

A small lie, but a necessary one.

"What? You got the part?"

Morris was taken by surprise.

"You're starting tomorrow night?"

When he stood suddenly, stars spun around his head. Lillian stepped forward to help him, but he brushed her away.

"I'm fine...fine. So, you're in the play now."

He needed to take control.

"Well, there's going to be a limit on how much you can be away from the house in the evenings, Lillian. You have a child and a husband to think of."

A wave of extreme dislike rolled through her. Who was *he* to tell her what she could and couldn't do? She stepped up on the first step to be at eye level with him. Before she could stop herself, long-stewed words erupted out of her.

"You treat me as though I'm a child... you tell me what I can and can't do. It's as though you think you own me, and..."

"Of course I own you, Mrs. Scharf. You're my wife. As head of the household, I make the decisions, and you'll do as I say. That's all. Done."

Lillian's heart pounded one sharp beat at a time. She needed to be careful. If she pushed against him too hard, he might actually tell her she couldn't be in the play... and then, what? A small steely resolve took shape beneath her breast bone.

"I'm sure the rehearsals won't take me away too much. Don't worry. I'll be here... but not tomorrow night."

With that, she turned, tromped up the stairs and opened Marcie's door. For a few moments all she heard was the rush of angry blood as it roared past her eardrums. But slowly, the child's soft breath and the peacefulness of the room calmed her. She adjusted the covers around her daughter's delicate shoulders, then heard Morris go into the bathroom.

In the pale light from the streetlamp, Lillian sat back in the rocker. She remembered Harold Winston's kind face, his gentle embrace. She replayed the moment when he kissed her neck, over and over.

From their bedroom, Morris cleared his throat in that particular way. It meant only one thing. For the first time since she had met him, Lillian's conscious response was instantaneous and powerful. She was repulsed by the idea of relations with her own husband, so much so that she considered lying to him about her time of the month. The problem was, he kept close track in his little calendar book of everything about her, along with other details of their lives together and who knew what else. Why had she thought, early on, that his habit of recording everything like that was endearing?

Marcie roused and turned her head in her crib. Lillian made some soft noises, adjusted the covers, smoothed the baby's head, then waited while she fell back into deep sleep. The strange thing was, she'd known all along what Morris was like. He used to refer to his little book frequently when they courted. She'd thought it meant he was organized and on top of things.

When she could put it off no longer, Lillian went into the bathroom to get ready for bed. Maybe if she took long enough he would fall asleep. In the mirror her face belied her present dilemma. She looked excited. She brushed her teeth, washed her face, spread lotion on her hands and elbows. What a wonderful change, to have the play happening in her life now. Well, nothing was going to get in the way of her being in that play... nothing.

When she slipped into bed beside him, Morris switched off his reading light then turned toward her. She saw his silhouette hover above her. Silently, he shoved her knees apart with one of his and without any other preliminaries, pushed himself into his good looking wife. After his abrupt satisfaction he rolled off her, turned away and fell asleep.

Lillian lay with a heavy heart – her eyes riveted on the street lamp outside the window where black branches moved like witches' arms in the windy night. Whatever the future did bring, she fervently hoped that it would not include relations with her husband ever again. She curled into a ball on her side, wiped away a rogue tear, and fell asleep to the sweet memory of Harold's embrace.

6

Every time she exhaled, Lillian saw her breath as she steered the buggy around bumps in the sidewalk. It was overcast but it hadn't rained yet – there was dampness in the air. She thought it must be just above freezing. Marcie lay on her back and watched tree branches pass overhead, tucked in in her wool snowsuit, so thickly padded that her unbendable arms and legs looked inflated. They made their way the seven blocks to Florence's house in record time – it was too cold out to dawdle.

When Florence opened her front door and saw Lillian on her porch, her freckled face broke into smile. The buggy with Marcie in it waited at the bottom of the stairs.

"Oh, Lil. I'm so glad to see you... Marcie, too. Come in

3

out of this cold right now."

The two women hugged. Lillian glanced around the street in the neighborhood but there was no one else in sight.

"Flo. There's something I have to tell you."

Florence looked closely at her friend.

"What's the matter, Lillian? Are you alright? Has something happened... to Morris? Have you heard about the stock market?"

"Ha. Funny you should ask, and it's *not* about the stock market. Let's get inside and I'll tell you."

While Florence held the handle of the buggy steady, Lillian lifted Marcie out and carried her, spread-eagle and stiff, into the house where she laid her on the davenport and undid many buttons and peeled layers off of both of them until they were down to their inside clothes. When she set Marcie on the floor, the toddler made a beeline for a basket of yarn that sat next to the rocking chair. Before she picked up the pink fuzzy ball, her eyes sought Florence.

"That's fine, Marcie honey. You can play with that. It's okay."

Marcie lifted the yarn ball out then plunked herself down on her large, diapered bottom and began to pull and unwind.

"Well, come on in the kitchen, Lil, and tell me what's going on."

Florence led them to the sink where she filled the tea kettle, lit the stove and put the water on to boil. After she got out the teapot and her nice tea cups and saucers she turned to Lillian who sat slumped on the stool and bit at a hang nail.

"Okay. What's going on? You look like something's definitely up."

Florence was Lillian's best friend, but Lillian wasn't sure how much to tell her. She had churned over Morris all morning and on her way over, and had come to a possible decision. She looked at her usual confidante, whose frizzy auburn hair and freckles looked adorable, as usual, even though they were the bane of Flo's existence. But those big brown sympathetic eyes always managed to pull Lillian in. She could tell her.

"Well, I'm in the Community Theater play. It's the Wizard of Oz and I'm the Scarecrow."

"That's good news. Why do you look so... not that thrilled?"

At the insistence of the tea kettle, Florence poured boiling water over the tea leaves, then put the lid on and snugged the cozy around it. She turned and leaned against the sink, slipped her hands into her apron pockets and waited. Lillian finally spoke.

"I don't know where to start." She bit her lower lip.

"But, the one thing I do know is that... well... I think... well... I'm thinking about leaving Morris?"

It came out like a question.

Florence's eyes got huge and round. Her face paled and one hand covered her mouth discreetly as it hung open. She couldn't talk. Slowly she shook her head no.

"Wha... why? Why on earth would you say such a thing, Lillian? Morris is a good man and a good husband... he's a mensch..."

Lillian cut her off.

"No. Actually, Flo, he isn't. He just *looks* that way to everyone... except me."

Florence gasped and bit her knuckle. Her words came out in a whisper.

"Why? Why? How could you do such a thing? What about Marcie?"

Surprised at the mention of the forgotten child, both women perked their ears up to listen for her. Dead silence. They rushed into the living room and found her on her stomach on the floor in front of the big chair with one arm stretched under, just out of reach of the cat.

"Here, honey. Let me get Mittens out for you to pet."

Florence grabbed the cat – Lillian, the girl – and they all went back to the kitchen where Marcie sat on a small stool next to the radiator for a short visit with the kitty on her lap. Florence set a cookie and a small glass of milk on the table for the little girl's next project. Then she turned to Lillian who gazed out the window over the sink.

"All right. Now, what are you talking about?"

She pulled Lillian around by her arm.

"Tell me more... please."

It was now or never.

"I can't stand him anymore, Flo. He's cruel. He doesn't have a feeling bone in his body. He thinks he knows it all and he acts like he's in charge of the world... and particularly, in charge of me."

Florence tsked and frowned, poured tea, then carried the cups to the table. They both sat. Marcie came over and wanted up, so Lillian set her at her place. While she slowly demolished the cookie into a pile of crumbs, Lillian continued.

"You just can't imagine what it's like trying to live with him. And, the worst thing is... is..."

A wary look crossed Florence's face. She squinted.

"Yes... go on."

"The worst thing is the way... the way... we have... you know... relations."

Florence gasped and a hand shot up to her neckline where she snugged the sides of her collar tightly together.

"What are you talking about? What could be wrong there?"

Lillian leaned forward across the table.

"I could be anyone. He doesn't even know or care that it's me he's... using. There's no connection between us, Flo."

Florence was aghast. She twisted the top of her blouse into her fist.

Lillian's voice rose with urgency.

"Is that what it's like with you and Sam... just a cold, necessary interaction between a man and a woman?"

Florence gave a quick, infinitesimal shake of her head... no. Lillian went on.

"I'm his receptacle, that's all."

A wince from Florence and sudden high color in her cheeks, but Lillian didn't notice.

"He's in his own world and I'm a convenience to him. It... I... I can't stand it any more."

She pushed away from the table and walked to the sink where she looked out the window into the gray day.

"I want love. I want a man to make me feel loved, not used. Listen, Flo. I know there's more inside of me waiting to come out. I know it. I'm a really good actress. Maybe I'm even great. And, it's all waiting inside of me. I want to be an actress...."

"Well why can't you be an actress and still be married to Morris? You have Clara. Can't she watch Marcie while you're at rehearsals?"

"Oh, it's so much more... hold on..."

While Lillian grabbed her cigarettes from her purse in the living room, Florence found a small cardboard box filled with sugar cubes in her cupboard and set it on the table in front of Marcie. As per their usual routine, first a cube went into Marcie's mouth, accompanied by a big smile for Flo. Then, the child carefully lifted one cube after another out of the box onto the table and moved them around and stacked them. It was one of the best diversions that Florence had in her house for the little girl. When Lillian returned, she lit up and blew her smoke into the back hall, away from where they sat. Florence leaned over the table toward her.

"So, why not just use Clara more to help you while you're in this play? Do you really have to leave your husband over it? Aren't you being a little overly dramatic?"

Lillian sought the right words to explain herself. She wanted Florence to understand, not condemn her.

"You know, my father loves to tell his cronies that it was a mistake sending me to college... made me 'too smart for my own good', he says."

She tapped her cigarette into the ashtray. Florence sat back. Lillian obviously needed a good listening to, and she could give her that.

"I don't know, Flo. I'm grateful that he even let me go. And, of course, what I discovered there is that I love acting. I'm a good actress. Actually, I'm better than just good."

"I believe you. I can't wait to see you in the play. But, why do you suddenly decide that you need to leave Morris? Just because you want to be in a play? Just because he's a little cold? Yours wouldn't be the first loveless marriage, Lil. Can't you work it out somehow with him?"

The gears churned inside Lillian's head. Florence was missing the point. The point was... the point was... how could she tell her about Harold Winston? What last night meant to her? How her life had turned a corner? If she wasn't careful, she would come across in a bad light.

Florence sipped her tea then raised her eyebrows questioningly. Lillian snuffed out her cigarette in the ashtray and leaned over with a hushed whisper.

"I need to tell you something... something private – completely private. You can't tell anyone, Flo. Not anyone."

Her look gave Florence the willies. She braced her hands on the kitchen table.

"Lillian Scharf. What have you done?"

Lillian took a deep breath and looked over at Marcie who looked directly at her while she moved sugar cubes around with her finger.

Her heart constricted, then lurched and throbbed.

"I met someone..."

51

Florence's lips formed a tight, straight line. A ring around them was suddenly pale white, almost blue. Again, she narrowed her eyes but she didn't say a word.

"I felt something I have never felt from Morris before... kindness. He's kind, Flo, and caring...."

It was too much for Florence. She stood and paced around her kitchen.

"Lillian Scharf! What are you talking about? You're a married woman. I can't believe you're saying these things to me. Jewish women don't just up and leave their husbands for another man."

Lillian tried again.

"Listen, Flo. You married a *good* Jewish man. Sam's a good man. He's kind and smart and patient."

Florence nodded agreement.

"But, Morris isn't. He's *not* those things... at least not with me. And, I don't want to spend the rest of my life married to a bully and a creep. I don't!"

She caught herself, lowered her voice.

"I've met someone who's different."

Florence wrapped herself in her sweater, then stood against the counter. She did not want to hear this.

"Are you telling me that you've been with another man? That you're going to leave your husband over another man? My own friend?"

While Lillian fiddled with a sugar cube on the table, Marcie slid off her chair and threw herself across her mother's lap. She squealed to get up so Lillian hoisted her up. What *was* she going to do?

"I haven't *been* with anyone. Well... I... he... and, I

don't know what I'm going to do. I think what happened last night showed me it could be different...."

Marcie nuzzled into her mother's neck and made squeaking noises as she tried to climb up the front of her. Unconsciously, Lillian returned the child to her lap over and over while she gritted her teeth, determined to keep the conversation going.

"Are you telling me that you didn't feel exactly the same the first time you were with Morris?"

Lillian was stopped up short. She *had*. She remembered his dark eyes, how good they had looked to her.

"Yes, true. But it didn't last. I can't pretend that I even like him much any more. He's absent, Flo. I think I must have made him up in my mind to be who I wanted him to be – this wonderful guy – instead of who he really is. And I can actually see that, now that we're married. Boy, you really do get to see what someone's like once you marry them."

Between their eyes, an understanding passed.

Marcie stood in her mother's lap and pulled, first at her ears, then her cheeks, then her chin, until Lillian noticed and snapped at her.

"Marcie, for heaven's sake, baby. I... here, don't do that to mama."

"So, you're telling me that something happened last night? What? What happened?"

There was no putting it off any longer. Lillian reached up, touched the nape of her own neck.

"He *did* kiss me... on the back of my neck... when he

was helping me on with my coat." She grimaced slightly.

The knuckles on Florence's fist dug into her front teeth. There were no words, but they sputtered out of her anyway in froggy bursts.

"You can't go out into the world with a baby and no husband. Lillian, that man *kissed* you! And, you're in the play and you want to leave Morris and... what would your mother say?"

Her face expressed horror, her freckled jaw dropped and hung. Then, she looked curiously at Lillian.

"Are you insane? Are you alright?"

She scrutinized her friend for signs of abnormality but, of course, Lillian looked fine. A little tired, maybe, but there was excitement in her. Lillian smiled, then shrugged.

"Oh, I suppose if I were to go through with this idea and really leave Morris, I suppose everyone would think I was crazy. But, I'm not. I think I'll *go* crazy if I have to stay married to him. Funny thing is, my mother tried to tell me. She knew."

"Your mother was smart."

They both nodded quietly.

"Well, what would you do? Get a divorce? Nobody gets a divorce – it's tawdry! What on earth are you going to do?"

Lillian – with an arm around Marcie, whose little fingers admired her necklace – carefully selected a cigarette from her gold case, tore a match from the matchbook, lit it up, exhaled and filled the back hall with smoke before she answered.

"Well, I can't do *anything* unless I have some money.

How would I pay for a divorce, even if I wanted one? I don't even have my own bank account. It's a joint account with Morris."

She held the cigarette between two fingers while she picked a fleck of tobacco off her lip.

"I can't get money out unless he signs, too."

A large heavy dark thing fell in a swoop through Lillian's insides. What was she thinking? There was no possible way she could ever leave Morris. None. She was stuck. With him. Forever.

"Lillian? Honey? Lil. Are you alright?"
Florence took a firm hold of Lillian's shoulder and put her face close to her friend's.

"I'm stuck and I want out, Flo. I really do."

"Oh, it just pains me to hear what a predicament you're in. And, I'm surprised about that side of Morris. Everyone I know thinks he's a mensch. It's hard to believe he's really like you say. For heaven's sake, don't tell him Harold kissed you."

She paused.

"But, what are you going to do?"

Lillian crushed out her barely smoked cigarette in the ashtray. It took her a few moments to know what to say.

"I don't really know... except for one thing. I know I'm going to play rehearsal tonight."

"Really? On Friday night? Shabbas?"

"I'll run home and fix his roast chicken. I'll be there for supper. He won't even notice that I'm not there later because he'll be at services. Plus, I told him last night that I was going."

Marcie pulled the gold chain around Lillian's neck until it broke. She held it up for her mother to see.

"Oh, for Pete's sake, Marcie. Here, give me that." She sought patience.

Florence sipped some cold tea.

"You're right, Lil. You'll need money to do anything. I have about thirty dollars saved up that I would be glad to give you. It's a start, anyway."

Lillian reached across the table to put her hand over Flo's and Marcie was squashed at the neck between her mother and the table. She choked out a yelp which sent Lillian backwards, one hand held high with cigarette, one arm tight around her baby. Both women chortled and Marcie laughed, too.

"You're such a good friend. Thank you, but I don't really want to take your money. Just keep it. Maybe I'll drive to see my father. Surely he can spare a little money for me. I know that my mother left some and I should be entitled to part of that."

Lillian didn't know what had happened to her mother's estate, or even how big it was, when she died two years ago. She pulled out another cigarette and lit it up.

An idea grew as she sat there. Tomorrow was Saturday. If Clara would watch Marcie, she actually could drive to Hampton to talk with her father. He had never been eager to part with his money, but this was for his daughter and granddaughter. Surely, if she explained it to him, he would understand her need to get away from Morris. He wouldn't want her to stay with a man who had no feelings, who treated her as if she were invisible. He wouldn't want that for her.

"Are you going to do it? Drive to your father's?"

Lillian took a long drag on her cigarette then crushed it into the ashtray.

"Yup. I think so. I'd better get home and get that chicken in the oven. I want a perfect Friday night meal on the table for Morris when he gets home. I don't want to do anything that might set him off. It's going to be tricky enough just getting out of there tonight."

The look on her face didn't convince Florence of much.

"You're gonna be okay, you know. I don't know what you're going to do, but, if anyone can do it, Lil, it's you. You're a firecracker. Remember your aunt's saying? You're the 'God-*dammit* Girl'!"

7

As Morris sat back in his easy chair, a huge, satisfied belch rumbled up and out from deep within. Lillian could certainly put together a fine meal. He picked up the evening's Globe Gazette and read the bold, black headlines: **Gigantic Bank Pool Pledged To Avert Disaster as Second Big Crash Stuns Wall Street: Largest Financial Powers in the City Meet After Day of Hysterical Liquidation Sinking Prices Below Thursday's**

He pulled his handkerchief from his back pocket and swept it across his forehead – another day with no customers. How many of those were there going to be? He read on:

After the stock market had come crashing down again in a veritable deluge of forced and hysterical liquidation, word sped through the financial district last evening that the largest banks in the city were prepared to exert their organized power this morning to prevent further disaster.

Arrangements described as "fully adequate" were completed at a conference at the offices of J. P. Morgan & Co. at Broad and Wall Streets...

Although no formal statement was issued, it was the consensus of those at the meeting that the worst of the liquidation is over and that a natural demand for investment stocks now available on the bargain counter should go far toward an immediate restoration of trading stability.

Well, good. Those fellows on Wall Street had better figure things out, and soon. Fluctuations made it hard on businessmen who worked hard to provide adequately for their families. The disruption in sales was not only inconvenient, it was typical. This crash could promote yet another depression in Iowa, the fourth since Reuben Scharf, his father, had begun to sell furniture, some clothing, and household goods in north Iowa twenty five years ago. The cycles were relentless, and since Morris took over the store after his father's death eight years ago, the instability of his gut always matched the market as it wavered up and down, especially down. Enjoyment from his meal was short-lived as his bowels churned uncomfortably.

Morris set the paper in his lap and listened to the water run in the bathroom upstairs. He was not happy that Lillian was going out for the evening. What kind of wife ran off to be in a play after supper? What would the boys from shul say if they knew Lillian was going to be out of the house so much – especially in the evenings? And especially tonight, with Friday night services. True, Lillian often didn't attend; but, still, it didn't look good.

He tossed the paper on the floor, rose quickly and a catch caught him in the side. He stopped halfway up, waited, didn't breathe, and it passed. Then he stood upright and climbed the stairs to find her.

Lillian, seated before her dressing table, peered in closely to scrutinize a blemish on her chin. Morris loosened his tie as he entered the room. He walked over and stood behind her, picked up the purple chiffon scarf off the back of her chair and ran it through his fingers as he watched her in the mirror. A myriad of possible things to say passed through his thoughts. When she looked up and met his eyes, her animated face surprised him. He spoke abruptly.

"We may lose a great deal of property, mostly the farms my father bought before the war... plus, some of our holdings in town, too. Things are going to have to change around here."

Lillian was wary.

"What do you mean?"

He pulled the purple scarf repeatedly through his fingers, ran it across the front of her neck as he stood behind her.

"We're going to have to cut back."

Unconsciously, he wrapped the scarf around her neck. He kept a hold of the ends.

Lillian sat stiffly. What was he doing with her scarf?

"What do you mean by 'cut back'?"

He gathered the ends of the scarf together and wound them around his hand – a snug collar.

"Well, let's start with household expenses. I'm going to lower your household allowance. I think we'll need to go to half of what I've been giving you. You can make do, can't you?"

He twisted the scarf once more around his fist. Lillian tried to swallow but couldn't. She forced a couple fingers in next to her neck and pulled. The look in his eyes frightened her. What was wrong with him?

Her mind worked fast. She could always get cheaper cuts of meat from Guttman's. She normally bought the best, though. That would definitely challenge her cooking skills. And, she supposed she could do some house cleaning, even though she loathed it. Her only fear was the potential loss of Clara. Time away from Marcie was essential to her and she needed Clara to watch Marcie during play rehearsals. She would clean toilets in a barracks if it meant Clara could stay.

"Yes, I can make it work."

He stared into the mirror at her and slowly tightened the scarf even more. Suddenly she couldn't breathe. Little stars appeared at the corners of her vision. She reached up and struggled to pull the scarf away from her neck.

"Morris! Stop! What are you doing?"

He let go of the scarf while Lillian coughed and rubbed her neck. She didn't know what to say. What was that all about?

Morris turned away, unbuttoned his shirt; spoke as though nothing had happened.

"I'm sure we'll be fine here at home."

She wasn't so sure – that look in his eye. She massaged her neck and calmed her voice.

"Why did you hurt me, Morris? Are you really that worried about money?"

Morris tossed his shirt over the back of the chair. He ignored the first question.

"Yes, that… and my mother."

Always his mother.

"She's gotten pretty used to the financial help I provide for her. I think with our cutting back here at home, I'll be able to continue to contribute my regular amount to her upkeep."

He continued to change out of his suit - blithely moved about the room – but didn't notice Lillian's raised eyebrow and set mouth. She gently massaged her neck and was about to find out more from him, then decided against it.

"I have play rehearsal tonight. I should be back by ten."

He turned quickly in her direction with a dark look on his face. It was a side of Morris that Lillian had never seen so much of before. He couldn't know about Harold so she assumed he was upset about the stock market.

"This is an unstable time, Mrs. Scharf. I don't want you out gallivanting around town. You should either go to services or stay home. Your child needs you."

The finality of his words struck Lillian. A vision of herself with a shield and sword, warrior-style, came to her. He would not take this away from her. She had ten minutes before she needed to leave in order to get there on time. She breathed deeply in and out once – calmed her insides.

"Listen. I already have the part in the play. Clara will put Marcie to sleep soon, anyway. Why don't we just take it one day at a time, Morris? I'll be home tonight by ten. And, you'll know exactly where I am. I can't quit now... that would make us look bad."

She said 'us' on purpose. What else could she say? What would soften him? Her outfit was ready, her hair was combed. She just needed to gather her things and she would be off.

Morris stood in front of his dresser and admired his visage in his mirror. If she reneged now that she already had a part, people *would* wonder why. As he spoke, he watched himself talk and obviously liked what he saw.

"Alright, then. But, be home by ten o'clock sharp, Lillian... don't be late. And, remember, we have dinner with the Goldsteins tomorrow night."

A surreptitious sigh of relief – she wasn't about to show him how worried she had been.

"Fine, then. I'll be home by ten, and I don't have rehearsal tomorrow so dinner with the Goldsteins will be fine."

She exited the bedroom without another word, said her good nights to Marcie, and fled her home with barely contained excitement.

8

Lillian hunched down deeper into her fur coat. The night was cold and she could see her breath. She carefully negotiated her way down the steep, narrow back steps, gathered her strength and heaved the garage door up, backed her car out, then got out and pulled the door back down. She always had a moment of euphoria whenever she put her car into first gear and drove away from the house, and tonight's pleasure was divine.

She drove slowly past the ball field at West Park but didn't turn in. The place was deserted except for one light on down by the warming house, where it was too early to make ice in the rink. She continued past the High School, where a couple of rooms were lit up and a man climbed into a car on the street at the bottom of the huge steps. Lillian pulled over at the edge of downtown, just past a streetlight in front of Olson's, the ice cream store, where she lit up a cigarette and watched people happily eat their ice cream through the steamed up windows. The night's darkness was so complete it felt like it could be midnight, but it was only 6:20.

Luckily, she had a play to work on during the upcoming long, dark winter nights. She saw herself stumble across the stage as the scarecrow. Maybe she could use burlap for the head covering of her costume.

A knock at the window startled her out of her reverie. She cranked down as a large face loomed into view. It was Leonard Shapiro, one of the businessmen in town. He and his wife ran the Hitching Post, a men's clothing store that leaned toward Western and casual. You could buy a good pair of blue jeans from him and even a cowboy hat, if you needed one. Leonard was a wiry, bowlegged little guy who always wore a thin mustache that followed the curve of his mouth.

"Hi there, sweetie. How's tricks?"

"Hi yourself, Lennie. Where's Sylvie?"

"She's inside in the Ladies'. Whadaya doin' out all by yourself tonight – leave Morrie home to suffer by himself?"

"He *is* feeling this stock market thing pretty hard. Aren't you?"

"You know, Lil, I never did put much stock in the stock market, heh-heh. Sylvia and I've saved our money at home. I think we're gonna do just fine."

"That's lucky, Len."

A motion at the corner of her eye caught her attention and she turned to look out the windshield. On the sidewalk, a young woman laughed at something her tall date had just said. She tucked her arm under his and they drew close together then sauntered off happily together. A vision of Harold floated into Lillian's thoughts.

"Where're you off to, Lil?"

"I got the part of the scarecrow in the play at the Community Theater. Tonight's our first rehearsal. I'm so excited."

"Well, that'll be something to see. You acted in college, right?"

"Yes, I did and I'm ready to get back into it. It sure will be a welcome change from diapers and the Ladies' club."

A skinny, drawn woman with pale white skin and black, black hair walked up and stood beside Leonard. She had deep creases around her mouth and when she smiled at Lillian, Lillian noticed a small chunk of red lipstick stuck on the corner of her front tooth.

"Hi, Sylvia. Did you get your hot fudge sundae, as usual?"

"Hi, Lil. Sure did – can't get through the week without it. How're you?

"I'm good. Listen, I've got to run to rehearsal. I'm about to be late. Leonard can tell you about it."

She put the car in gear and was about to pull away when Sylvia leaned in and spoke in a hushed voice.

"I hear that Harold Winston is directing. What a hunk. Too bad his wife is such a...."

A car motored by with young people hanging out the

windows. They shouted and called out to someone in Olson's. Lillian strained to hear what Sylvia said, but she couldn't make out the last words.

"What, Sylvie? What is Harold Winston's wife?"

"She's crazy, Lil. She's been in the state home for years. They never had children, but I heard she became very childlike before he took her to Independence."

"Yes, I heard something about that. It surely is a sad thing."

"Yeah, but it means he's unencumbered, Lil." She winked. "He's such good-looking guy, too. Maybe I should..."

Before they could talk more, Leonard stuck his head in close to the window, said goodbye, then pulled his wife away from the car by the sleeve of her coat. Sylvia's mouth made an "O" and she laughed, then she waved in Lillian's direction and turned to walk with Leonard.

Lillian had never really done anything seriously wrong before, so she was surprised to find herself being pulled (in her own thoughts, at least) toward a potential path of wanton self-destruction. That was just one way to look at it, though. She had a serious hunger for more of the flattering attention that Harold had lavished on her. Those were some powerful feelings that had passed between them. She was pretty sure that he looked forward to seeing her tonight, too. He obviously had needs of his own in this little drama.

She gathered her nerve, then pulled the car out into the street and made her way to the church.

Inside, Lillian hung up her coat then leaned down to tug

at the back of her skirt where it clung to her stockings. When she stood up, Harold walked by, engaged in conversation with a woman whose arms moved around as fast as the words flew out of her mouth. As they passed, he lifted an eyebrow and dove his eyes down the front of her and then back up. She nodded a hello to both of them.

If acting wasn't her favorite thing to do, Lillian might have walked out right then. There was time to turn around. Nothing too serious had happened, yet. She could just go home, spend the evening next to the radio with Morris.

Lillian looked into the crowded fellowship room from the hall. Why did she have to be married to a man like Morris when there was someone who made her feel the way Harold Winston did? She preferred the second.

"Lillian, good to see you."

Millie lumbered up like a friendly puppy. Her hips poofed up and out over the waistband of her skirt and churned and rotated freely when she walked. It was true her head looked a little small on her oversized body, but her personality far outweighed her physical appearance.

"Hello, Millie, it's good to see you, too. Let's get this play going, eh?"

Nothing organized was going on yet, so they both leaned up against the counter to the kitchen.

"So, Lil, how're things at home? How's Morris?"

Lillian threw her a sideways look. That woman could see into her.

"Honey, I'm referring to the sorry economic state of our poor nation. People stand to lose some money in this mess. I know your husband. He takes his responsibilities seriously."

Millie was one of the few businesswomen in town so she knew a couple of things about the financial goings-on. She had a boutique where she sold things that she and others had made, all of which were one of a kind; colorful aprons, pots she had thrown with deep purple or blue hued glaze, and an array of paintings and painted boxes. Lillian, who loved handmade things, had gone in there on occasion to purchase gifts.

"Well, yes, he's worried about money. He has properties that he will probably lose because people won't be able to pay their rent and then he won't be able to pay the mortgages."

"I suspect it's probably worse than he's letting on."

She threw Millie a sly look.

"Oh, I know it's worse than he suspects, Millie. It's... definitely worse."

Millie laughed a big hoot.

"Lillian Scharf. What are you talking about?"

"Millie, have you ever done something that you knew – going into it – was wrong, and that it might wreck *the way things are supposed to be*; but you couldn't stop yourself from doing it?"

"Well, honey, who's '*the way things are supposed to be*' are we talking about?

Lillian nodded her head slowly.

"You know what I found out the other day? Do you know about the prayer that men say when they daven in the mornings?"

"You're talking about Jewish men, right?"

Lillian hugged herself. She had never talked about this with anyone before.

"Yes, right."

"No, I can't say that I do. I don't subscribe to any religion, you know."

"I know, Millie. You go through life so freely... not constrained by the rules and regulations that the rest of us are supposed to follow."

Millie paused and tilted her head thoughtfully.

"I just use my conscience and my heart. For me, that's a good combination. I'm not real prone to having a man, or anybody else, tell me what I should think or what I should do."

Lillian knew what Morris' response to that would be. He would say that no man would want Millie anyway – she was too fat and ugly. Whenever Lillian saw Millie act in a play or even just interact with people in regular life, she was drawn to her. There was an honesty and kindness about her that Lillian admired – a rare authenticity. She liked the way Millie thought about things and wasn't afraid to speak out. But, in her affairs, she went through life more like a man than a woman.

"So I don't have a particular way except for listening to myself in a situation. Because, really, I don't care what people think of me. I know what's good for me, and I know I'm a good person."

She breathed on her fingernails then buffed them against her ample bosom.

"Now, what's this about Jewish men?"

People started to form into small groups in the room but

Lillian didn't want the conversation to end. She leaned over closer to Millie and talked directly into her ear.

"You know that I read a lot and ask the rabbi lots of questions about Judaism and religion?"

Millie shrugged.

"They're good subjects to question..."

"When I asked the rabbi what it is men are praying about in the mornings when they daven, he told me that one of their prayers is about thanking God for making them a man and not a woman."

Millie raised her eyebrows.

"Gee, what an honor."

Lillian was aghast. She looked around to see who might have heard.

"Oh my gosh, Millie. You say such outrageous things."

"I think most men think that way – that they're God's gift, and that being a woman would be a fate worse than death – not just the Jewish ones."

Lillian couldn't believe this conversation.

"Well, in my experience, the man certainly has carte blanche on running the show. Sometimes Morris acts like I'm his daughter instead of his wife. He is definitely the one in charge in our little family."

"Welcome to the second night of tryouts...."

Jane called the evening to order.

Millie gathered her bag off the floor and took a step away. She turned and looked directly into Lillian's eyes.

"Lillian, dear. Who's in charge of your life, anyway? Him... or you?"

Before she could investigate the implications of Millie's

bomb, the try-outs bloomed into full gear. At Harold's insistence, Lillian took a seat in the back of the classroom. By 9:15, she had seen more than enough Dorothys, tin men and cowardly lions. She excused herself before Harold was finished writing notes, to go to the Ladies' room.

As Lillian peered into the mirror at yet another new blemish on her chin, she listened from behind the restroom door as people left. A couple of voices exchanged good-byes then the final few footsteps clomped up and out the door. She had no other option now but to go out to meet her fate. Once more, she checked her face in the mirror. An excited, bright-eyed woman looked back and she couldn't help but smile at herself.

This is one of life's bigger moments. Here I go.

The lights were all still on when she stepped out into the deserted hallway. She shifted her coat from one arm to the other and walked quietly over to the doorway of the Fellowship Hall. Across the room, Harold squatted beside a bench with one knee down and read some papers.

As she watched him, Cupid intervened. Perhaps a minute went by. Lillian imagined his rise off the floor, his approach to her – arms outstretched – then being slowly enfolded in those arms. She leaned her head against his chest and felt his heart pound.

Harold stood up then, still across the room, just as Lillian shuffled her shoe. He turned and saw her, and when he smiled, she felt heat creep up her neck and across her face.

"Hey, beautiful... I was hoping you'd stay."

He stood where he was, as did Lillian.

"I couldn't go, Harold. I thought we should..."

She wasn't sure what she wanted to say. Should they talk? Should they go out for a bite to eat together? She didn't really want to do either of those things.

Harold set his papers down, finally, and walked toward her. His eyes asked a thousand questions, and hers reflected her own version of them back to him. She dropped her coat. There was a moment before they came together – a brief hesitation. Then, they gathered into each other's arms and bade farewell to the past.

They kissed with a hunger that surprised them both. Lillian's lips kept perfect time with Harold's. They were singing an opera together with their mouths. All she wanted to do was answer his every question. Could he understand this communication? Something was pulling at her all the way up from her toes.

He gently pulled his head back. Lillian saw that he had tears in his eyes. He looked deeply into hers.

"You are the answer to my every question, Lillian. I could sing with you forever."

Now, Lillian's eyes filled up and overflowed. He cupped her face, wiped away the tears with his thumbs. When he kissed her again, Lillian felt something in her change, something fierce. She *wanted* this. She wanted him.

She knew after one minute of kissing Harold that her life had just turned another corner, and she was happy to do it. Suddenly, there was light before her. In her life, the only feeling this strong had been Marcie's birth. She could not deny this.

"Lillian?"

Harold looked around them at the fellowship room of the church with its harsh light. Someone had left a red stocking cap on one of the benches.

"Can we find a better place? Hmm?" The kitchen? The office? Upstairs?

He leaned his face close to hers and peered into her eyes.

"Let's go see. Come with me."

They held hands as Harold led them up the stairs, through the church. He stopped in the darkened sanctuary and pulled her around into his arms.

"I've found you. I don't want to let you go."

His voice nearly broke.

"I'm right here, Harold. I'm not going anywhere."

They kissed. Lillian felt both protected and too excited to speak.

She took his hand as he led them to a door at the front of the sanctuary. Behind the door was a small office room, where vestments, like silent sentries, hung on hooks on the wall. A flood light from the parking lot offered just barely enough light through the window to see around the room. They both peered into the near darkness. There was a desk and a small sink with a towel hung beside it. At the same moment their eyes fell onto a cot snuggled into the far corner. A small pillow at its head reflected blue shadows. Lillian's heart thumped in her chest. Harold leaned down – whispered in her ear.

"Come, my dearest. Let me love you."

She let out a small gasp, then turned to face him.

"This is not something I do lightly, Harold."

Her eyes searched his.

Harold looked up into the air above Lillian's head. He stood for several moments with a pained look on his face. The angles of his bones made deep shadows around his eyes. Then, he relaxed and looked down at her with great tenderness.

"Lillian…you are the most beautiful woman I have ever met. And I'm not just talking about how good you look. I fell in love with you when I watched you audition. The 'you' we all see fell away and who was left was a smart, talented, intense and just plain amazing person. Such an understanding you have… of beauty, of goodness, of all the things I have needed and searched for, for so many years. I want to pay homage to your beauty, Lillian."

She raised an eyebrow... that sounded a bit too good to be true.

"And," he confided in a whisper, "I can't wait another second to love you…"

Lillian had a big decision to make but she didn't want to make it. She wanted these moments badly – she wanted them never to end.

She couldn't stop now – she didn't want to. Whatever happened now, she was willing to face the consequences. Her legs turned to jelly – she lowered herself onto the cot.

He kneeled beside her – brushed her bangs back off her forehead. They kissed, and she became more and more lost in the universe of Harold. He gently planted kisses on every tiny bit of her exposed skin then proceeded to expose more.

Lillian could not form coherent thoughts. Images flowed through her mind as though driven by high winds. She saw Morris pass by, eyes angry. All the people she knew floated into her vision and right back out again. Harold had uncovered all of her – all of her. She lay naked in the dim light – sleek curves of light and shadow – and writhed imperceptibly before him.

"Harold, take your shirt off. I want to feel your chest."

She was drunk with the scent of him. He knelt beside where she lay and slowly removed his clothes. They exchanged smiles and she waited impatiently.

Then, he leaned over and planted kisses down the front of her until his mouth reached its destination. Lillian saw flowers on hillsides, castles on mountains and ocean waves lap against the shore.

His tongue probed a question; she arched toward him with her answer. He went to work in earnest, his arms laid over her protectively. She threw her head back, gathered tension and excitement until she exploded – laughed and cried. Harold ran his hands lightly over her as she calmed.

When she could talk, she turned her face toward him and met his bright, eager eyes.

"Harold, how long are you going to make me wait?"

With that, Harold climbed carefully onto the cot and, with sureness, entered her. In an instant, they were both swept up by a gigantic surge. Lillian saw bright lights go off like fireworks explosions. She clung to Harold, clambered to get closer and closer. They rocked together – rode the powerful waves past all boundaries. He shuddered as the raw force of nature pounded through him, and came with an involuntary moan that matched hers, and was magnificent and helpless in his release.

Lillian stroked the back of his head and a huge tenderness toward him enveloped her. She wrapped her arms and legs around him.

So this is what it's all about.

9

Lillian wasn't perfectly sure what her plan should be, but she knew that in order to make her own life happen, she needed money, and the only person she knew who had some, and who might give her some, was her father, Max. If she asked Morris for money, he would want to know what it was for, and she wasn't prepared to tell him, yet.

When she awoke Saturday morning, Morris had already left. She found Clara with Marcie in the playroom. The child stood to kiss her mother, then squirmed away to play with her blocks.

"So, I'll be out most of the day, Clara, and then Mr. Scharf and I are going out for dinner tonight. It shouldn't be too late."

"Don't worry about a thing, Mrs. Scharf. I'll get the laundry folded while she naps."

"Oh, thank you so much, Clara. I do appreciate you, you know."

"I know that, ma'am."

Lillian gathered her purse, the lunch she had made for herself and a jar of water with a lid, and left the house.

She drove south out of town on the newly paved section of highway 65, out past the fairgrounds and the cemetery. Dark, heavy clouds hung like giant dirty pillows in the sky – low slung undulations that spanned the horizon. The day was gray and cold.

Farmers and their families headed into town for supplies; lots of pick up trucks, even a few horse drawn wagons. For miles, Lillian's was the only car that traveled in her direction.

Broken and tattered cornstalks stood askew in the fields which fanned away from her as she drove. Occasionally, she passed a farmstead, raked clean and sitting in wait for snow. Sometimes the ripe smell of cows seeped into her car as she passed them, with heads hung, in paddocks of nearly frozen mud.

Lillian inhaled her cigarette and let her eyes wander the distances. It relaxed her.

Their faces alternated in her mind: Harold's urging eyes; Morris' mouth, set hard... Harold's tender hands; Morris' look of disapproval last night as he turned toward her from where he stood near the fireplace.

"It's late, Lillian. It's ten twenty-three."

She had redone her makeup, so she knew she looked presentable. It's just that she wasn't a very good liar.

"There were so many things to work out... first rehearsal, you know."

She gave a little smile as millions of bubbles rose from her belly and crawled up the front of her.

There was a flutter along his jaw line. He couldn't know anything. She searched for something to say.

"You sent Clara home?"

"Of course."

"Do you need anything? I'm pretty tired."

"No. I'm fine."

When Lillian walked over to her husband to kiss him good night, he took a hunk of the back of her hair into his fist, pulled her head back a few inches and held it there. He leaned back, himself, to see her better, then squinted. The monotone of his voice belied the compliment.

"This play must be good for you, Lil. You're radiant."

She reached up, ran her fingers through her hair then conjured a fleeting smile.

"I love it. It feels so good to be acting again."

A moment went by.

"Alright, then. Goodnight."

"Goodnight."

As she walked up the stairs to bed, Lillian took a deep breath, then let it out. *Did he suspect anything?*

She was still awake when he climbed into bed beside her. He turned her on her back and with no preliminary preparation, entered her and used her swiftly and thoroughly – drove home his possessive dominance. He was, after all, her husband, and it was not only his right, but his duty to God to have her.

The experience was not much different for Lillian from all the others, except for one small thing. In her heart, she held a secret glowing image of the person who might be able to rescue her from her immutable life sentence with Morris – the beloved whom her heart had always sought. It felt like hope, and her eyes filled with tears. She rolled over, curled up into a ball and wondered where it would all lead.

A few miles out of town the road turned to dirt and Lillian stepped on the gas. The car's heater chugged out a thin stream of warmth – barely enough. She tucked the wool blanket around her thighs and thought of last night, of Harold.

He rolled gently to the side of the cot near the wall.

"My God, woman, what have you done to me?"

"I didn't do this any more than you did, Harold, and you know it."

She turned on her side to look into his face. His eyes were shining and crinkled in humor and happiness. In the dim light, Lillian could just make out his smile. He stroked her hair back off her face and ran his palm over her cheek. His touch was strong and gentle. He spoke in a whisper.

"I don't want to let you go... ever."

Lillian's breast was filled to the brim. She didn't want to say what came to her.

"There's so much standing between us, though. I have a

whole life, you know; a daughter, a husband."

At that, Harold closed his eyes. His mouth formed a line that turned down at the corners.

"I know, my dearest. But those things don't make me want you any less."

Lillian slowed her car as she passed through the town of Rockwell. It wasn't much more than a crossroads that sat in a vast cornfield with a few scattered houses, a general store, a small white church and, at the end of town, a bar. She didn't see anyone about on this chilly October morning. Just outside of town, at a wide point in the road, Lillian pulled her car to the side and parked. She lit a cigarette and sat and smoked with the window cracked – back in his arms.

"It's the same for me, Harold. It feels like the beginning of an opening has happened that could propel me into a freedom and a happiness I've only dreamed about."

He readjusted his body so that he could hold her in his arms. They both moved carefully on the cot, shifted their weight to adjust themselves so Lillian's head rested on his shoulder. Harold reached over her to the floor for his shirt, which he spread on them for warmth. Then they lay together for a few minutes, excruciatingly happy.

"Harold?"

"Hmm?"

"Is there any way... for us... to be... together?"

"Are you supposed to ask me that after just two days?"

She quickly pushed up onto her arms.

"Don't you want that too?"

"Lillian, my beauty... this isn't going to be easy for you. For me, there's no doubt... I know I want to be with you. But, what do *you* want?"

What did she want? Was this a legitimate question? Did it matter what she wanted? How on earth could she even believe for one moment that she could move from one life into another? From a predictable, cold, suffocating marriage with Morris to a loving, warm lifetime embrace with the man in whose arms she lay? The chasm gaped huge before her – she didn't want to think about it.

"What *I* want, Harold? I'm not so sure that even matters."

"Does it matter to you, Lillian? Does what you want matter to you?"

Up until her marriage, Lillian had always known what she wanted, in all aspects of her life. Well, she wanted to marry Morris, for heaven's sake. What went wrong?

"Harold, I think I picked my husband for the wrong reasons."

"Like what?"

"I wanted the security of a nice home... and a husband who made enough money for me to live in a respectable style."

"That doesn't sound like a wrong reason to me."

"Yes, but, remember, I had to pick a Jewish man – there was just no other option. And, there aren't that many of them around here in Iowa. Morris seemed like a good pick before we were married. And, he courted me... flattered me. I thought he was wonderful."

Harold unconsciously ran his hand lightly over Lillian's hip, up and down her side.

"I don't mean to pry, but, if you want to tell me, I'd be curious to know what changed."

"I don't mind, Harold. It feels good to talk. I'd say that the first thing that happened was that his mother refused to come to our wedding."

"Off to a great start, hmm? Why?"

"Oh, it's because my family is all German Jews, and his is all Russian. And, well, German Jews aren't good enough in his mother's eyes."

"Good enough? For what?"

She stared up at the ceiling, rolled her head from side to side.

"For her son to marry, that's what."

Lillian sat up, crossed her legs and cast an oblique shadow against the wall.

"And then, this is unbelievable – even to me – she came on our honeymoon!"

"Your mother-in-law went on your honeymoon? That's unheard of. Why?"

"Because Morris is attached to his mother, that's why. And God forbid he should have another woman in his life who matters."

"It sounds like she's attached to him, too."

"Oh, I get so tired of trying to measure up for his mother. I should know by now that it's never going to happen."

Lillian opened her car door and ground her cigarette butt

soundly in the dirt at the side of the road.   That woman was the least of her problems.

The driving was mindless. She passed three cars and a couple of wagons headed in the opposite direction. The loose steering meant she could turn the wheel broadly from side to side and the car hardly weaved. It didn't take long before she dreamed of Harold again.

They lay quietly together. Lillian felt peaceful but wary.

"What else, Lil?

"Do you mean, what else changed? Because I'll tell you... maybe nothing. Maybe this is the way a marriage is... when the husband dictates a schedule for what he wants to eat and won't deviate from it... when he cuts his wife's allowance in order to keep his mother's the same..."

Her fingers dug into his arm.

"When he takes... *takes*... what is apparently his pleasure and forgets to notice that there's another human being in the room."

Her voice shrieked out the last few words, then she sat up and buried her face in her hands, not exactly crying.

Harold rested his hand on the back of her neck, caressed her gently. In his wisdom he said nothing.

"I can't do it any more, Harold. I can't pretend that everything's alright when it isn't. I don't want to spend the rest of my life as the invisible servant of Morris Scharf."

She sat with arms clutched around her knees.

"I know I vowed to be the perfect wife, and I have certainly done my best to fulfill that promise. But, Harold, how can I go back to him and pretend that I don't know you? That I'm happy with him when I want to be with you?"

For a few moments… silence. Harold sat up against the wall and pulled Lillian into his embrace.

"I want you, Lil. But I don't want you to be hurt."

"Ha. This is going to be the mess of the century. Do you really think that Morris is going to sit back and let his wife run off with some man who he doesn't even think counts in the big scheme of things?"

"I don't count? What do you mean?"

"Well, Harold, if his mother didn't think enough of me to come to her own son's wedding, do you really think that he's going to acknowledge a goy as any real threat in his life? He'll probably just turn around and laugh."

"Oh, I don't think so."

"No, I don't really either. But, how on earth am I going to extricate myself?"

Lillian tried to get up to put her clothes on, but Harold kept his arms wrapped around her. He nuzzled into her neck with his nose.

"Can you remember my arms around you tomorrow? Can our being together here tonight help carry us both to our next rendezvous?"

Lillian looked thoughtfully into Harold's beautiful green eyes. She smiled.

"I think you're worth what I know I'm in for."

His eyebrows shot up.

"I think you're worth it, too, my dear."

Then he smiled and they kissed in a long and luxurious embrace.

The tiny town of Sheffield was tucked into the cornfields amid a stand of hardwood trees and blue spruces. Lillian slowed to drive through what looked like a theater set: tidy little white clapboard houses, two storefronts and a miniscule church. How would someone have come to live in such a place – so small, so remote? She sped up to negotiate the last few miles to Hampton.

There was some hustle and bustle going on in the little town by the time Lillian arrived. Farmers' wagons were tied up to rails up and down the two blocks of Main Street and a few cars were parked diagonally around the square. Bundled-up people hurried through the cold to get their shopping done.

Her father's store sat on a corner that faced the courthouse and Lillian saw customers go in and out with their purchases. She parked where she could keep an eye on the store and lit another cigarette. Her fingers tapped the steering wheel repetitively.

If she came right out and told him about Harold, her father would blow. She knew that. Maybe she could tell him she needed money. But, for what? To leave her husband? Lillian rolled her window down about two inches, stuck her cigarette out and flicked the ash off. Well, that's what she needed it for, wasn't it? She might as well be straightforward about it all. He would want a reason. How about: I like him less every day.

Lillian harrumphed. She opened the car door, dropped the cigarette and smashed it out. Who knew what she was going to say to her father? Better to get it over with.

Surely there was money somewhere that she must be entitled to. She pulled her coat around herself and crossed the street to her father's store.

Max Rosenheim always took his morning constitutional at 8:15. He walked for fifteen minutes and arrived at his store, Rosenheim's Haberdashery, promptly at 8:30. That gave him thirty minutes before he opened to tend to paperwork. He walked briskly this morning, head down into the wind, while he ruminated about the perilous state of his and the world's financial affairs.

Myra Fishbeck, the early waitress at the diner, paused from her sweeping and watched from across the street as he came to a stop in front of his store. Max gave the illusion of being a square man – height and width comparatively – so that despite his short stature, he was a man of heft. He ran his hand through his graying hair then smoothed his white mustache.

Before he walked into the store, he rearranged himself until his spine was correctly aligned – shoulders back. After all, he was a highly respected citizen in Hampton – a successful haberdasher – who, due to the consequence of being born Jewish, was not eligible for a seat on the town council. Nevertheless, he had the honor of calling the mayor a close personal friend.

Max entered the store, breathed deeply the old familiar scent and hadn't yet closed the door when he froze. His skin suddenly rose up off his body. He let out a moan. For, there she stood in front of him, clear as day: his dead wife, Rosa.

Max could neither move nor speak. He turned his head to look out the window just as Myra walked back into the diner. He was still in Hampton... still in his life. His eyes flew again to where he had seen his wife moments before. There she was. Her beautiful dark eyes beseeched him. One of her hands rose in supplication toward him, then she disappeared.

Max's heart pounded painfully. His hand grasped at the front of his coat as he staggered toward a chair near the hats. There he sat for several minutes as he waited for his heart to slow down.

What could it mean? Maybe he hadn't really seen her. Maybe the trouble with the market was causing him to see things that weren't really there. It was probably just one of those optical illusions. He had worried a great deal lately... too much, probably. He needed a break. He should get out of town for a few days... spend time in Mason City with Lillian and Morris. It would be good to see his granddaughter, Marcie. A shame she hadn't been a boy. Still, she was cute.

Several minutes passed. When he finally looked up, he saw only the calm, orderly interior of his store as it awaited the day's transactions. By the time the tinkle bell over the door announced Laverne Johnson's quest for the perfect handkerchief to embroider, Max Rosenheim's morning visitation was nothing more than a wisp of dissipated memory.

The morning passed quickly as a constant stream of customers came and went from the store. He sold a bowler to Karl Anderson, who had a remarkably small head for such a tall man. And, he had the devil of a time when he measured Jacob Berger for a new suit. The man had to weigh three hundred pounds. The material, alone, would cost a fortune – at least twenty dollars. Luckily, Berger was from a well to do family on the East coast and was happy to spend whatever it took to keep himself spiffed up.

Max hadn't given another thought to the strange and frightful apparition of the morning, nor had he thought again about travel to visit his only daughter, Lillian. When the door opened just before noon, however, and she walked in, something moved through Max that felt like a mighty nudge from God. All the hairs rose up instantly on the back of his neck. He stood firmly where he was, behind the wood and glass display case, both hands splayed on the top, fingertips pressed against the glass.

Lillian pulled her scarf off and unbuttoned her coat.

"Hello Father. You look like you've seen a ghost."

Max struggled for equilibrium. He rubbed his palms down the front of his apron then came out from behind the display case. With each passing moment he gained composure.

"Hello, Lillian dear. Wonderful to see you... just wonderful."

He took her by the shoulders and kissed her on her forehead, then wiped his own with his handkerchief.

Lillian lifted the cover off the jar of horehound candy that had sat on the counter since she was a little girl. She deftly extracted a piece and slipped it into her mouth.

10

The late afternoon light angled in through the west windows. Morris leaned forward, turned off the radio and stood up from his well-stuffed living room chair. His black hair glistened as he smoothed it back on both sides of his temples. These were certainly troubling times. A man could lose his footing easily if he wasn't careful. A firm hand was what was needed. He and his brothers must not go soft on the renters up in the north end of town. A good portion of the Scharf income came from those people. He did not want to lose his enviable way of life because of a misstep, nor did he want his mother's well being to suffer because the economy was so volatile.

Morris was a determined man. He could get things done

if he set his mind to it. Hard work – and always a prayer of gratitude for the Almighty, the holiest One.

He paced across the room, then turned and paced back to his chair, head bent forward – pulled along by his thoughts. When the telephone rang he shot straight up and listened for Lillian or Clara to answer. After six rings he walked to the kitchen alcove and picked up the heavy black receiver.

"Yes? Morris Scharf here."

A large, slow, autumn black fly hurled itself against the lower left corner of the kitchen window, over and over. Outside the window, the afternoon waned.

"I have a person-to-person long distance call for Mr. Morris Scharf."

The operator's voice was high and nasal.

"This is Mr. Scharf. Go ahead and connect me, Lavonne."

"Yes sir, here you go."

Morris heard some clicks and then the line opened up.

"Yes, hello. It's Max. Max Rosenheim. I'm calling long distance. Can you hear me?"

He shouted into the phone.

"Scharf? Are you there?"

To Morris, his voice sounded small and crackly.

"Yes, Max. I can hear you fine. How are you? Are you alright? Is everything alright?"

The fly landed deftly on the window glass then crawled slowly upward, diagonally. Morris wondered how it could stick to the glass like that.

"No, sir. No, sir. I am not alright. No, sir; not one bit."

Morris began to speak but was interrupted by Max. Every time he tried to say something, Max sputtered into incredulous diatribe so that Morris finally just stood silent – waited for him to calm down. The fly buzzed around in furious persistence. He caught a few of his father-in-law's words.

"... wife... Guten himmel... divorce... crazy...."

Finally, there was silence at the other end. Morris heard Max breathe heavily into the telephone.

"I can't quite make out what you're saying, Max. Could you say it again?"

He leaned against the kitchen counter and checked his cuticles. One had a little piece that needed to be bitten off, which he tried, unsuccessfully, to do. Max's voice was churlish, gruff. This time Morris heard clearly.

"Your wife, who is my daughter, tells me that she wants to leave her husband."

The telephone fell off of Morris's shoulder where it had been cradled with his chin. He fumbled with it in his hands before it fell and clattered to the floor. He saw the receiver on the floor and heard his father-in-law's tinny little voice come out of it. Although he tried several times to pick it up, he was unable to do so – unresponsive arms, unresponsive hands, couldn't squat down to get it – frozen.

"Everything okay in here, Mr. Scharf?"

Clara ran her hand along the banister as she hurried down the stairs. In her other arm she carried a small bundle of dirty clothes. She saw Morris stare down at the receiver.

"I heard the telephone ring, then I heard... Here, let me get that for you, Mr. Scharf. Here you go."

She eased herself over to pick up the phone, then handed it to Morris, who steadied the receiver up to his ear. He cleared his throat and spoke in a register an octave below where he usually talked and twice as loud.

"What, Max? What? What are you telling me? Are you referring to Lillian, my wife?"

"Who else, you damn fool. She wants to leave you... go off and have a different life. Says you're not, what was her word, not compatible."

"This is the most ridiculous thing I have ever heard! We don't have any problems. She never said anything like this to *me*."

Morris, whose face and ears had flushed bright red, turned to see where Clara was. She had gone on down the basement. He could hear water run at the laundry sink.

"She says you already know."

Max sounded fed up and disgusted.

"How would I know?"

There was a loud buzz in Morris' head.

"You don't know? I suggest you make it your business to find out immediately, Scharf."

"What did you tell her?"

Morris tried to stay calm but a waver came into his voice, which made him angry.

"What do you think I told her? I told her to remember her place. She's a married woman, for God's sake. She has no business thinking like this. She should be a good wife and mother. That's what she was put on this earth for... not for gallivanting around doing plays. That was all fine and good before she was married, but not now. Did you tell her that it was alright to be in a play, for God's sake? Who's in charge in that house, anyway? Do you hear me, Scharf?"

Morris looked for the fly but couldn't find it. He noticed a light colored scuff mark on his shoe which would need to be tended to right away. Outside, he heard children's shouts. He struggled to swallow before he talked, then he could barely get the words out - he was so humiliated.

"Yes, sir... I'll take care of it. I surely will. You have nothing to worry about, Max. This is surely just a passing fancy. Don't worry about a thing. I'll set things straight here."

Dots of perspiration shimmered on his forehead. He couldn't think of anything else to say.

"Stand up and be a man, Scharf. It's your God-given duty. Women need to be handled, not coddled. You don't want her besmirching your good name in that town. You've worked too hard for that."

Morris spoke slowly and carefully in his deepest possible voice.

"Yes, sir. You're right, sir. I'll take care of everything. Thank you for calling."

They both mumbled a goodbye. Morris' hand trembled as he lowered the receiver into its cradle. Clara clomped up the basement stairs and Morris fled upstairs to his bedroom. He heard Marcie wake from a nap down the hall. He shut the door and paced frantically while he smoothed back the hair at his temples over and over.

He couldn't believe what he had just heard. Lillian had

told her father that she wanted to leave him. After all he had given her... a Cadillac convertible, a beautiful home, financial security, even a daughter! And this was how she fulfilled her wifely obligation? By bypassing him and going to her father?

Morris clenched his fists until they shook, then dug them into his temples. He wanted to strangle someone, but instead he turned abruptly and kicked the wall. Then he kicked it again, harder. This time he made a dent in the plaster and several chips crumbled to the floor.

11

On the road home from Hampton, Lillian pulled her car over and parked under a giant elm next to a cornfield. She leaned back against the fender and puffed up the collar of her raccoon coat. As she sucked hard on her cigarette, her hands shook. Tears of frustration and anger squeezed out of the corners of her eyes. She blinked hard a couple of times to chop them off, then blew smoke out in a fast, narrow cloud. On all sides of her, as far as she could see, lay ragged empty cornfields, and here and there, dots of farmsteads with miniature windmills standing guard.

She squinted off into the distance but all Lillian really saw were her father's eyes, filled with rage, as words – like nails – hurled toward her.

"You're a crazy woman!   What do you think?   Do you think you're free?   That you can decide now I'm tired of my husband, I'll go do something else?"

He paced back and forth in front her, arms flying.

"It is not for you to decide.   You are a married woman, Lillian.   It is done.   This is your life.   It is God's will."

"But, you don't even go to synagogue.   How can you use that argument with me?"

"God's will is God's will, whether I go to shul or not!"

Lillian heard the oo-oo-ga of a car horn out in the street. Inside of her, a hundred thousand words rolled over the edge of a high cliff and fell off into darkness.

"You have nothing to say here.   There is no argument for you against the covenant you made with God.   You married Morris before God.   I was there, I witnessed it. And, so did your mother, may she rest in peace."

And, as he said it, Max remembered what had happened that morning.   He remembered the vision of Rosa, her hand reached out toward him.   Beautiful Rosa, with that look on her face... she wanted something.   She was asking him for something... but, what?

Max's face blanched.   He found a stool, sat unceremoniously, his feet wide apart, and absently pulled the handkerchief from his front pocket.   He patted his forehead, his cheeks and then his neck.   Oh where was Rosa now?   She would know the right thing to say.   He looked up at his daughter who watched him closely.   She was temporarily out of her mind.   That was all.   What did Rosa want from him, on today of all days?   That he should be a mensch? That he should stand up and be a real man – the head of the family? Could it be that simple? Of course. That was it. She came to him from where she lived now, with God, to remind him of who he was – who he must remain. She was always a good wife.

"I am a man of God, Lillian. There are certain things you do not change."

He jabbed his pointer finger into his fleshy thigh.

"No daughter of mine is going to tell me what you are telling me."

Lillian sought an avenue. Her words sounded weak to her, but she said them anyway.

"It's 1929 Father, and we're not in the old country, either. Things are changing. A woman can get a divorce..."

Max roared up out of the chair.

"Shah! You are insane! Do you hear yourself?"

His nose was inches from hers. She smelled his hot breath and saw vivid red veins branch off in the whites of his eyes. She leaned back imperceptibly.

"You may not speak again these terrible words to me, your father, who provided for you and educated you. What? So that you could marry a fine man and grow up to come here today to tell me that you're tired of him, that you're not... what... compatible? *Compatible?* This is not a thing a wife decides."

He stood as a behemoth before her. Inside, Lillian faded rapidly backwards – rushed away from where she stood in the store with her father – to a pinpoint far back behind her that she could see coming from a long distance. She saw herself as she stood on a high windy ledge. Below her: fire, blackness, nothingness. She could execute a perfect swan dive and go away forever. It would be easy. But, a black bird with white shoulders and long tail feathers cawed down to her and flew toward the land from over the abyss. Her eyes followed it, her head turned. The bird's shadow moved across the ground and Lillian followed tentatively, pushed forward by the unseen hands of her mother.

Max had her by the shoulders. As he jostled her, Lillian's eyes filled with tears. He ranted.

"... I say no. The answer is *no*... I will not give you money. You go home right now and behave properly. Do you want to ruin everything your husband has worked so hard to provide for you?"

She searched a full sphere of possible answers in an instant.

"That isn't why I'm doing this...."

Max peered questioningly at her as though she were feeble minded. Lillian held on to the memory of Harold's arms around her. She remembered the feeling of her mother's prodding from a moment ago. She thought of Marcie, who waited for her at home. There would be no money from her father. She would have to think of some other way.

"I'm trying to...."

The bell over the door to the store tinkled loudly and both Lillian and Max instantly shot upright to a more formal stance. An old, stooped woman with a cane fought with the door to get in. Max turned to his daughter, scolded her with a finger and a harsh whisper.

"I don't want to hear another word about this... ever... not ever. Think of your mother..."

Beside her car, Lillian shuffle-kicked the gravel under her right shoe until there was a bare spot, then dropped her cigarette butt and ground it out.

Her mother knew. She knew what kind of man Morris was and she knew it long before Lillian did. Max had accepted Morris from the beginning, pulled him immediately into his confidence, treated him as the son he'd never had. He loved for the two of them to share a good cigar together. Her mother, though, had seen Morris for who he really was.

She missed her mama so much. How could she possibly go through the world without her? Lillian covered her face with her hands and let grief erupt out of her.

As she cried with her head bowed, a flock of Canada geese honked toward her from far off over the fields on her right side. She found a hanky in her pocket and wiped her face and blew her nose just as the heavy birds passed directly overhead, squabbling to each other. Neck craned back, she held them in her sight then turned and watched them slowly disappear over her left shoulder.

Her life was an old dishrag about to fall to pieces – just a few threads left. The idea of driving back into Mason City put a glob in her stomach which joined the downward pull that was already there from her visit with her father. The only way she could get herself into the car to drive somewhere was the thought of Florence. There was still time before she needed to be home, if she drove fast, to visit Flo.

After Lillian tucked the blanket in around her thighs and pulled onto the road, she revved the engine harder and higher before each release of the clutch, and relished the power.

12

Florence thought about getting up to fix dinner. She had an onion, a couple of potatoes and a piece of leftover roast. A hash sounded good to her. It was getting colder this afternoon – something hot and oniony would help her feel better. She and Sam had sat in their chairs for over an hour to listen, first, to Amos and Andy and then the news, which, mercifully, Sam had slept through most of. The financial news was ominous and Florence was worried. They didn't make much between them to begin with. Sam was a carpenter, a handy man, and she worked at Hedberg's ladies wear as a sales clerk. They managed alright and had a small savings account, but if people stopped buying fancy clothes or if no one wanted to pay someone to have work done on their house or business – which Florence could understand under the circumstances – well, she didn't want to think too hard about it. It gave her a stomach ache. Yes, a hash it would be.

She wound her frizzy auburn hair up in a knot, secured it the best she could with hair pins and had just tied her apron on when there was a knock at the back door. Before she got there to open it, it opened on its own and Lillian's face peeked around the edge.

"Oh, I'm so glad you're home, Florence."

She smiled through her teary eyes.

"Lil, what's wrong? You've been crying. Come in, come in. I'll make us some tea. Here, don't let the cold in."

Lillian hurried inside as Florence closed the door after her. They hugged, then Florence filled the teakettle at the sink and set it on the burner which she lit with a match. The cozy smell of sulphur and gas filled the room and took away some of the chill of the late afternoon.

Lillian settled herself on the kitchen stool in the corner. Here she was again: Florence was the lion tamer, Lillian was lion.

"I can't stay long, but 'thank God for you' is all I can say, Flo."

"Well, why don't you tell me what's going on. Things are a mess everywhere, I'd say. The radio... ah, I don't even want to think about it."

"Oh ho, don't I know. Everyone's getting worried about money... me, too. You have no idea how deep my problems are. I don't even know where to start."

The teakettle quickly worked itself up into an insistent whistle. Florence cut it off, then poured the boiling water into a chipped teapot and watched the leaves swirl.

"Where are you coming from right now? Where have you been today?"

She carried the teapot to the table with a hot pad. Lillian left her coat on the stool and joined her.

"My father... I drove to see him. I was asking him for money to..."

"Whoa, Lil. You went to see your father? Today? You drove to Hampton and back today?

"Florence. You're my best friend, and I have something to tell you that you can't tell anyone else... okay? Not even Sam."

Florence gingerly picked up the lid of the teapot to check on the tea. Then she poured them each a cupful. If Lillian was going to entrust her with a secret, she wanted them both fully armed – fingers warmed around the delicate cups. Flo put a teaspoon full of sugar into hers and stirred slowly. She looked directly into Lillian's big brown, red-rimmed eyes.

"Shoot."

Lillian picked up her cup by the handle and held the other side gently, blew across her tea, then took a sip. She paused to listen for sounds of Sam in the house. They both heard muffled snores from the living room so she leaned forward and whispered to her friend.

"I'm thinking of..."

She bit her lower lip and pulled it through her teeth.

"I'm pretty sure I'm going to leave Morris."

"What? Seriously?"

Florence looked around quickly, and carefully set her teacup back in the saucer. She leaned in toward Lillian.

"What on earth? Why? How? Does this have anything to do with Harold Winston?"

Lillian's mouth formed a straight line as she nodded her head solemnly up and down.

"Yes. Yes, it does. I'm... I..."

Her eyes opened wide. She looked stunned, then her face crumpled into a heap. Florence tsked and efficiently pulled a clean hanky out of her apron pocket. She handed it across the table, reached out and put a strong hand on the shoulder of her friend, then waited while Lillian snuffled and blew.

"Things have happened, Flo. I've been with Harold..."

Florence crossed her arms. She was beyond knowing what to say.

"What do you mean... been with?"

"Don't tell anyone, please. I haven't told anyone else. I have to talk about this."

She looked up at the ceiling.

"Yes... *been* with."

Florence took a hold of the edge of the table with both hands.

"If you mean what I think you mean, oh my gosh, Lillian. You've committed adultery! How could you?"

"Listen. If you knew what Morris is really like you wouldn't be so surprised."

Florence shook her head 'no'. She spoke in a hushed

whisper.

"What could be so bad that you would do such a thing – that you're ready to leave your husband? Think about Marcie, for heaven's sake. What will this do to her? A woman can't just leave her husband. What will you do? How will you support yourself?"

She nervously ran her fingers around the edge of the saucer. Lillian stared into her teacup.

Florence spoke quietly but sternly.

"Morris is a fervent Jew, Lillian. You know that. He isn't going to go for this for a second."

"Yeah, I know. He prays every morning to thank God for making him a man, and even better, a Jewish man. It's the highest calling on earth... the Jewish male."

She waved her hand around in the air in dismissal.

Florence sat back and crossed her arms, head tilted, and spoke hesitantly.

"Well, of course it is... I don't understand, Lil. You know how things are. You're Jewish. You married him. He's the boss. The man always is."

"I don't feel that Jewish any more, Flo. I think I've gone beyond religion. I feel like I've turned a big corner in my life...."

Florence leaned in toward Lillian and whispered harshly.

"I think you've gone completely nuts, Lillian. Nobody talks like you do. What could possibly be so bad about Morris that you're talking like this? He's a good man. Don't you remember how hard he pushed to allow women and children to sit with the men in the Friday night service?"

"I don't know why he did that, either. I think it's because his cousin, the rabbi's son in Cleveland, told him to... probably so he would look good to the congregation."

"Well, it doesn't matter. He did it. He's a mensch. Everyone knows that about Morris Scharf... he's a good man, Lillian."

Lillian poured herself another cup of tea. She chewed the inside of her cheek. Yes, Morris always did look good to everyone else in town.

"Let me see if I can explain this to you."

She looked directly into her friend's eyes. Her left eyebrow lifted.

"Does it bother you at all that only a man can touch the Ark or the Torah?"

Florence didn't hesitate.

"No. Why should it?"

"Why don't women count equally with men for a minyon? Why is our touch dirty to the holy relics?"

Florence took a hold of the collar of her dress and closed it tightly around her neck. She looked around again to make sure no one heard.

"You are thinking dangerous thoughts. A woman shouldn't be talking about the things you're talking about, Lillian. What's the matter with you?"

"He doesn't even notice that I'm there when we... you know."

She fluffed her hands toward her abdomen.

"It doesn't matter that it's me, Flo. You don't know what that's like, but I'll tell you... it makes me feel invisible. To him, I'm just a female, to be the boss of. I'm below him."

Lillian's fists were clenched on the table as she leaned across in a conspiratorial whisper.

"Something big is happening. I'm seeing some things I've never been able to see before."

Florence shook her head 'no' quickly and repeatedly. Her mouth tightened into a pucker. To calm herself, she opened the icebox and took out the plate with the meat on it. She sat down again at the table with her cutting board and a sharp knife, trimmed fat off the cold roast and chopped the meat into little cubes. Florence worked slowly and carefully, looked up often at Lillian who had that squinty eyed, determined look on her face.

Lillian talked off into the distance, past Florence.

"I don't know if I'm going to leave Morris for Harold. I certainly couldn't stay in Mason City and do *that*. And, I'm not sure that I want to jump so quickly from one man directly to another, even though Harold *is* dreamy. You can't believe how dreamy."

Her eyes filled again with tears.

"I don't know what I'm going to do, because, first of all..."

She blew her nose and wiped her eyes.

"... I don't have any money of my own, and until I do, I can't really do anything, and I really want to be in this play, and I really *do* want to be with Harold, and... Do you mind if I smoke?"

She dug through her purse.

Florence sorted through the onions that sat in an old

wooden bowl on the counter. She chose a large, firm, yellow one then turned toward Lillian.

"Of course not, honey. But, how can you just throw away your husband like that? You have so much together, a beautiful home and a beautiful daughter? Do you really want to be alone in the world with no one to love you?"

An easy question for Lillian.

"I'm alone already. There's no partnership. Well, there is, sort of. We look good as a couple. The house runs smoothly. But, I might as well be alone and... I don't have one cent to my name."

The reality of that statement sent a shock through Lillian. She sat and smoked, amazed by her own predicament.

Florence handled the onion, passed it from one hand to the other.

"But don't you and Morris have an account at the bank?"

"Yes, but, surprise, surprise, we both have to sign if I want to take money out of it. And you know what? He doesn't need my signature if he wants to make a withdrawal. Why is that?"

Florence pursed her lips, set the onion on the table.

"That's right. That's just the way it is. That's the way the world is set up."

She picked up two potatoes that sat on the counter and scrubbed them with a small brush at the sink.

"You can't take on the whole world, you know. This is 1929. Think about it. We've only been able to vote for ten years. And the way things are now, with the government and the whole financial thing? It's not good. You can't expect real equality, Lil. It's just not going to happen... at least not for a long, long time. Can't you just be happy with your beautiful home and Marcie?"

Her eyes opened up.

"What are you going to do about Marcie?"

"Well, after the last few days, I don't think anything can be the same as it was... ever. I didn't go to college so I could end up with someone like Morris. I want more. My life can be fuller and better, I know it can. I can feel it."

Florence spoke softly.

"And Marcie?"

"Marcie?"

Lillian dropped low.

"Oh...."

She sat for a moment. When she looked up at her friend, she smiled off one corner of her mouth.

"Marcie will be just fine as long as she's with me. I'll keep her with me."

With arms crossed in front of her, Florence leaned her head way back.

"You know I love you, Lil. But, I can't for the life of me figure out how you're going to do any of this."

Lillian exhaled and filled the small kitchen with smoke. She sat, elbows on the table, one hand up. Her thumb rubbed against her middle finger and she looked off as the cigarette burned. Florence patiently diced the potatoes. Lillian smoked her cigarette down to a nub and neither woman spoke until they heard Sam get up from his chair in the other room. Immediately, Lillian was all business.

"I'd better be going. We're supposed to go out for dinner tonight."

Her friend questioned her with a look that said: what are you going to do?

Lillian gave her shoulders a little shrug and made a grimace back.

"I don't know..."

Florence winced. She lowered her voice.

"Let me know what you're up to, Lil. I'll help you any way I can, even though you're not making much sense right now. We should talk some more tomorrow...."

From the hallway the women heard a gravelly voice.

"I can tell it's Lillian by the smoke."

Sam, a short man with black curly hair and wire rimmed glasses, came in and waved his hands to clear the air.

"Hi Sam, I'm just leaving."

Lillian got up, swung around the table, flung her coat over her shoulders and stopped at the door.

"Have a good dinner, you two. Talk to you tomorrow, Flo."

And, out she went.

Sam smiled to himself as he checked to see that the back door was closed.

"She's a feisty one... she have somethin' cookin'?"

Florence kept her head down – chopped onions. When she looked up at her husband to answer, tears ran down her cheeks. She hunched up one shoulder in answer: don't know.

13

When she sat down in her car again, Lillian noticed the sandwich that she had made in the morning on the seat beside her. She picked it up, unfolded the waxed paper around it and took a huge bite. The late October afternoon had slid away. It was cold and nearly dark out. She tucked the blanket in around her legs and started the car, but she couldn't get herself to drive home yet. A bite of her sandwich – a roll with a piece of meat, a slice of cheese and a pickle – helped her think.

How could she see Harold? It was Saturday night and the next rehearsal was not until Monday. Maybe she could go for a drive tomorrow and casually pass by his house.

She knew he lived somewhere on the east side of town, over by Jefferson school. He would whisk her inside where they would talk. Lillian saw them kiss in his kitchen, then tip-toe into his bedroom. She didn't want to wait to see him until Monday night.

After two bites, the sandwich lost its appeal. She put the car in gear and drove away from the curb. On the ride home from Florence's, Lillian considered every possible way she could think of to get away from Morris. Maybe she could take a long trip with Marcie to visit Pauline, her mother's first cousin in Chicago. Pauline always included an invitation for a visit in her letters to Lillian. If only she had some money to buy a train ticket.

The truth was, though, now that she was in the play, Lillian didn't really want to leave. What she wanted was her exact life as it was now – without Morris in it. Well, that was absurd. Morris was the reason she had such a beautiful home, her sweet baby girl and all her nice things, as well as a certain respect shown her in town. Lillian had to admit that she enjoyed having lots of money at her disposal, and Morris encouraged her to buy nice things. It was a complete reversal from her childhood where both of her parents had been careful with what little money they had. Now, because of the financial crisis in the country, she didn't know what was going to happen with their money. No one did.

Lillian didn't look forward to dinner with the Goldsteins. Hy and Morris would surely discuss the country's financial woes. Well, maybe she could learn a few things if she listened to them. The stock market wasn't something that she cared much about, but it would be good to know a little bit, anyway.

The thing she wasn't looking forward to was having to see Morris in a few minutes. Ever since her first rendezvous with Harold on Thursday, Lillian could hardly stand to be around her own husband. He had gotten icky so fast. In just a few nights she had gone from: if not happily married – at least in the ball game, to: not being able to stand the sight of him.

She had tried for more than three years to see everything between them as alright. She had made compromises in her own life in order to be the good wife that Morris expected her to be, the good wife she wanted to be. Her dream of becoming a real actress was interrupted and probably gone altogether. And, now, the thought of Morris sent a shudder of repulsion through her. Compared to Harold, well, there was no comparison. How could she possibly change her life?

In the early evening, as she drove over the Cedar River bridge, Lillian saw warm lights emanate from the windows of the houses she passed. It looked like everyone had a happy, cozy home life except for her.

A few things were becoming clear. When she had followed her heart to be with Harold, it was as though she had walked through a door. And, life goes forward, door after door, relentlessly, like ocean waves. Her life had definitely turned a corner. She didn't have much choice but to go in the new direction. Lillian drove slowly to prolong the trip home.

Morris turned away from the wall he had just kicked a large dent in and heard Lillian's car pull up in the driveway. A visceral shock rolled involuntarily through his body. He stepped quickly across the room to check his hair in the mirror, picked up his brush and gently smoothed the sides and top back. He took a good look at himself, shimmied his shoulders to undo the tension, then braced his feet solidly. She had some answering to do.

In his own eyes he saw a brief flicker of fear that provoked his anger again. Who was she – his wife – to betray their intimacy to her father? Her father! He looked back at the mirror one last time and smoothed his shirt in the front. He would handle this. His father-in-law was right: he was the head of the family. It was his God-given duty to set her straight.

As he heard the garage door close, Morris corrected his posture and did his best to hold down the anger that kept a small tremor alive in him. He descended the stairs. At the bottom, in the cupboard where he kept the liquor, Morris moved bottles around until he found his scotch. With shaky hands, he poured himself a couple of fingers, threw his head back and felt it burn all the way down.

He met her as she was coming in the door – his voice lurched from him.

"Where have you been? What have you been doing?"

Lillian cringed at the harshness. She ducked her head, closed the door behind her and unbuttoned the top button of her coat. What was he so angry about this time? Could he possibly know about Harold?

Morris braced his hand high on the door frame and

trembled as he hissed at her.

"Answer me! Where have you been?"

She couldn't say a word. She kept her eyes down and reached for a hanger off the rack. Her voice, when she finally spoke, came out quiet and low.

"I drove to see my father..."

He cut her off.

"What for? Why did you drive to Hampton today?"

In a split second, Lillian's mind grabbed at possibilities: Tell him the truth, make up a story, just tell him about wanting money but not what for... He was obviously upset... best not to dig a hole for herself that she couldn't get out of.

She tried to sound blasé, but the tension he exuded was catching. Lillian felt it roil in the pit of her stomach. He knew something.

"Why are you so angry, Morris? I can visit my father if I want to."

She adjusted her coat on the hanger then hung it on the rack.

"Don't we have dinner with the Goldsteins tonight?"

A small trickle of pinched words found their way out of him.

"Yes... we... have... dinner... with... the... Goldsteins. Why your *father*?"

His eyes bulged with fury.

She turned to look at him and was instantly frightened. His eyes pierced hers.

"So, tell me now, Lillian, what were you doing at your father's... asking for money? What for, huh? *Huh*?"

Beads of sweat broke out on his forehead. He crossed his arms.

He knew. He knew that she wanted to leave him. The entryway felt claustrophobic. Lillian tried to brush past him to make it into the den, but he caught her by the arm and turned her roughly around. Her heart flubbed around recklessly in her breast. He leaned in close and sneered, threateningly.

"You want to leave me. That's it, isn't it? Why?"

She nodded no, tried to back away. He had a bruising hold on her upper arm.

"Morris, stop. You're too angry. Let's talk about this later... when you've calmed down."

"You bet I'm angry. I'm angry, alright. I'm..."

Clara cleared her throat behind them and they both turned abruptly to see her. She stood a few feet away in the den with a frightened Marcie in her arms. The child squiggled out of Clara's arms and ran to her mother, clasped her around the knees with both arms and whimpered. Lillian, whose whole body shook, scooped her up, and was glad for the interruption. She buried her face deep into Marcie's neck, breathed in her baby's sweet scent, then exhaled a huge sigh.

"Everything's alright, baby... mama's home. Thank you, Clara. We should be ready to leave for the evening in half an hour. Can you get Marcie's dinner started? I think there are some cooked vegetables...."

While Lillian calmed herself with talk, Morris stomped out of the room. She heard him climb the stairs and slam the door to the bathroom.

The two women locked eyes for a moment.

"Come on, Clara. Let's feed this baby. I want to spend a few minutes with her before I leave again."

"Yes ma'am... I'll be here all evening, you know."

"Well, yes, of course. We had arranged that you would be, didn't we?"

"Yes ma'am. Just so's you know."

Clara nodded solemnly at her.

A grateful Lillian carried Marcie into the kitchen where she maneuvered her into the high chair, then she and Clara put together some dinner for the two of them. When she could put it off no longer, Lillian went slowly up the stairs to get dressed. She slid her hand along the banister and wished... well, wished she were anywhere but where she was.

Her father had telephoned Morris. It was unbelievable. Her own father had betrayed her. She didn't want to face Morris, but there was no other way. What a mess she was in. What a day this had been. Lillian could hardly drag herself up the stairs.

She heard Morris close a drawer in their bedroom so she slipped into the bathroom. In the mirror she didn't see her usual happy face. She looked tired. Whatever was next in her unmapped life, Lillian didn't know. She leaned over and doused her face with cold water, then buried it in the towel for what she wished would be forever. Morris cleared his throat loudly from the bedroom, which she knew was her invitation. Nothing to do but go in to see him...

Lillian opened the door to the bedroom at the same

moment Morris yanked on it from the other side. She stumbled in, leaned forward and he backhanded her heavily across her temple. Lillian saw a bright flash then felt the pain, but she made no sound. She flew into the dresser, gouged her hip deeply into the sharp corner and rammed her shin against an edge, then slumped down to the floor between the bed and the wall. He was immediately over her, fist raised, ready to hit. Lillian wrapped her arms around her head, curled up and shook... waited for the blow. Instead, he gave her a sharp kick with the toe of his shoe high on the back of her leg.

His voice was a ragged whisper.

"You are my wife. You will not think again about leaving me. Do you understand?"

Lillian could not make a sound. She hurt everywhere.

Morris leaned over her – clipped his words.

"In this house *I* am in charge. You mind *me* and do not go anywhere without *my* permission. Do you hear?"

He stood up and smoothed his hair back with unsteady hands. He caught a glimpse of himself in the mirror and stood up straighter.

In her painful cocoon, Lillian had a lucid thought. *He really thinks he owns me.* She tried to roll onto her knees to get up but her hip hurt too much.

Morris was calmer.

"Alright, then... Let's get ready to go. We're due to meet them at Costa's in fifteen minutes. And..."

He carefully removed his jacket from the valet and hung it over his arm, then jabbed a finger in her direction.

"Remember what I said."

He left the room and closed the door firmly behind him. At the bottom of the stairs, he found the scotch, poured himself another shot and threw it back.

Lillian thought that if she lay there for a few more minutes, maybe the pain in her hip would subside. Her shin didn't bleed, she had checked, although it had an angry red dent like a pothole and stung badly. She laid her hand on her forehead and pushed her bangs aside. Her breathing slowly returned.

Now she was determined... whatever it took.

14

With slow, careful movements Lillian got up, got dressed, put on her makeup, brushed her hair and descended the stairs to join her husband, who was starting the car for their evening out. She kissed Marcie good bye.

"We'll be back by eleven, I'm sure, Clara."

Clara's mouth was a pinched frown. She nodded, then set the small tin cup she held on to the baby's tray.

"You're okay, Mrs. Scharf?"

Lillian's eyes filled with tears. She looked down at Marcie who spilled milk on purpose. Clara grabbed a rag – Lillian took the cup. Neither woman said anything, but as their eyes met, Lillian knew that she had an ally in the house, and it helped.

It was a long walk out the back door and down the steps to the garage. She used great force of will to open the car door, then got in and sat down gingerly. Morris cleared his throat, an old habit of his that suddenly repulsed her. She looked straight ahead.

They drove in silence for a few tense minutes until Morris finally took a quick sideways look at her. He shifted slightly in his seat; his voice was low and menacing.

"Don't you ever try anything like that again, Lillian, do you hear me?"

No response.

He reached over and clutched her arm fiercely, then shook her once, hard.

"I'm talking to you...."

She stared straight ahead, wondered which thing he was talking about. A tiny voice rose from a tiny place.

"Okay."

"Keep your father out of our business. What we do is none of his business. *I'm* in charge in this family, not him."

He shot a look at Lillian while he steered over and around irregularities in the road. They were in the Scharf and Sons Furniture company car – a Chevy. Whenever they hit a bump, they bounced in unison on the springy seat.

Two more minutes went by. As Lillian watched the road disappear in front of them in the headlights, the scene in her bedroom ran over and over in her mind. She had been taken completely by surprise. Who was this man?

The numb shock from what had happened less than half an hour ago began to wear off. Her head throbbed, and spots all over her lower half radiated stinging pain. She didn't want to be going to out to dinner and she especially didn't want to be going out with the Goldsteins. They were an older couple and Esther Goldstein didn't care one bit about anyone else, she only liked to talk about herself.

Morris tipped his chin up.

"This play, this community theater play you've been going to in the evenings..."

His voice took on a swagger.

"It's over, Mrs. Scharf. You will stay home with your family where you belong. No more play."

Being the man of the family was an important job. If only the financial situation weren't so unstable – he slapped the steering wheel a couple of times – everything would be under perfect control.

In her seat, Lillian, shrunk down to the size of a dot, was dying inside. Her soul gasped for breath, clung to the edge of her being. She felt her last hope of happiness recede away. He might as well have punched her directly in the stomach.

Dinner went automatically for Lillian. They arrived at the restaurant, greeted the Goldsteins, ordered dinner. Hy pulled a bottle in a paper bag out from under the table and surreptitiously poured a shot for everyone. She sipped her way through hers while Morris downed three. Esther and Hy kept even. By the time the food arrived, Lillian's head spun. She couldn't talk very well, which was fine, because she didn't want to anyway. This had to have been the worst day of her life. Well, the day her mother died was horrible, too.

At the table, the other three talked about yesterday's stock market crash.

"This looks like the big one to me, Morrie. You set up pretty well?"

Hy puffed harder and harder on his cigar until the end glowed from deep within.

Morris answered almost too fast.

"Oh yes... yes... I'll be fine. This isn't the first depression we've had to get ourselves through, Hy."

He straightened his bow tie and spoke as though, to Lillian's ear, he was trying to convince himself of what he was saying.

"My brothers and I are planning to extend credit. You know, credit with interest. That way, people can make payments on a purchase over time and we'll make more in the long run."

Hy sat back, ruminated – mouthed his cigar wetly.

"I see what you mean. What percentage do you think....?"

Lillian turned to Esther. She knew that if she could start the woman talking, she wouldn't have to say another word for the rest of the evening.

"What are your children up to? They're in high school now, right?"

And... she was off. Lillian heard about the baseball team, the debate club, the band, the latest styles the girls wore (shorter dresses yet) and much more about Esther's female problems than she cared to know. Her dinner, a slice of spare rib with mashed potatoes and gravy, sat uneaten as it cooled and congealed through the megillah of Esther's life.

She didn't care about any of it. Everything hurt. She wanted to go to bed and was thankful when they finally said good night to the Goldsteins and got in the car to drive home.

Morris worked a toothpick between his teeth as Lillian watched the darkened houses slide by. He drove slowly, satisfied with his meal and with the outcome of the evening. Hy Goldstein was a savvy fellow; he knew some good tricks for how to hang onto money.

Lillian, her body turned toward the door as much as possible, sank further and further into quiet. Her head pounded, her heart sadly kept time. She was drained, exhausted – could hardly remember the beginning of this day. Her universe was so small and so frighteningly big, and she was definitely alone in it tonight.

Out above the trees, light gray clouds flew over the moon.

As they turned off of Maple Drive onto Woodshire, they saw several cars parked in front of their house and another one, a police car, in the driveway. Morris pulled up and jumped out. Lillian sat and watched, immobile. A fat policeman and Morris leaned over something that was smoking on their front lawn. One of the other men held a torch aloft, another wrote on a tablet with a pencil. It all seemed far away and dreamlike to her. Let them deal with it. She'd had it. She laid her head back against the top of the seat and closed her eyes to try to soothe her headache.

The car door opened and startled her. It was one of the policemen.

""Scuse me, ma'am, but you'll have to come out here. We need you as a witness."

She gathered what strength she had left and walked over to where the men looked down at the grass, but didn't understand at first what she saw. The wind blew the smell of gasoline and smoldering ash into her face. A six pointed star the size of a tabletop had been burned into the grass. She stepped away onto the front walk then looked toward the house. The torch threw moving shadows which made it hard to see, so she called them over.

"Bring the torch, here, quickly, please..."

The men stood directly in front of the house and shed light on the yellow paint as it dripped slowly down the Scharf's oak door.

$$$ DIRTY JEW $$$ THIS IS YUR FALT $$$

Morris was beside himself. He grabbed the torch and walked up close to the door.

"This is an abomination! Who did this? Those bastards! They're not going to get away with this..."

The fat policeman took off his hat and scratched at his scalp. Some neighbors had gathered at the edge of the lawn and along the sidewalk. They stood and murmured among themselves.

"Yes sir, Mr. Scharf. This is a bad, bad thing. We'll find out who did this and take care of it, sir.

"Well, you'd better. I'm an honest citizen of this

community. My father was Reuben Scharf, of Reuben Scharf and Sons Furniture. I pay taxes. I..."

A body disengaged from the small crowd that had gathered and a man stepped up onto the lawn.

"What is this, Morrie?"

It was Leonard Shapiro. He and Sylvia lived four houses away on Maple. Sylvia kept a keen watch of the goings-on in the neighborhood from her front window.

Morris folded his arms firmly in front of himself. His mouth was drawn tightly down.

"Look at this. This is an outrage!"

Lillian was beyond doing anything, so she stood on the front walk and watched everyone else. The police proceeded with their report, asked questions, walked around the house and looked for clues. Sylvia, in her mink stole and pajamas, sidled up, tsked.

"There are some real idiots in this town, Lil. They're just a bunch of thugs who get their jollies by running around committing vandalism."

Lillian looked at Sylvia who appeared to be far away, behind dirty glass. She knew the woman had said something, but nothing intelligible registered. Would it be too rude to go inside and lie down? She hobbled over to the front step and eased herself down onto the flagstone, folded her arms on her knees, laid her head down. Giving birth to Marcie hadn't been as hard as this day was.

"Come on, honey. Let's get you inside."

Sylvia put an arm around Lillian's shoulder, pulled her up, offered her small body as counter weight to Lillian's.

"You look like you need to go to bed."

In the house, Lillian sent Clara home, then moved with stealth up the stairs, into the bathroom and into bed before Morris went up. She pulled the quilt up around her neck and spent a few extra moments to find a comfortable position, curled on her least injured side.

She saw the vast, October cornfields span away from her in a fan as she drove by. Long rays of cold sunshine illuminated a golden tree whose leaves stood poised to drop....

A firm grip pulled her onto her back. He said nothing, but wedged his knee between her legs and dragged them apart. She didn't resist, she didn't participate. He was despicable. He drove his penis into her, dry. With her eyes closed, Lillian looked over cornfields in the crisp autumn air... a whiff of wood smoke, a lone duck flapping past, a sunset sending a warm glow her way, her mama, her baby.

15

Lillian felt the lift as she came awake and then, immediately, the leaden weight of her tender body. With eyes still closed she sensed that she was alone in the bed, but she didn't move. She listened for another few minutes to make sure. With great care to her right hip, she rolled slowly onto her back and stared at the ceiling.

It was early. Marcie was still asleep and Morris was at basketball. He went every Sunday morning to play with his pals in the Jewish league, many of whom had played together since high school. He would be gone all morning.

She watched the branches outside the window wave their slow, creaky answers to the wind. Every time a strong gust came up, a thin, high, lonesome whistle sounded through the window frame.

The only thing Lillian knew for sure was that she needed to leave, and soon. She needed to talk with Florence to figure out a plan. How could she get out of the house for good, with Marcie, and without Morris knowing they had left? He would never agree to a separation. It was impossible, but that didn't matter. She'd do it anyway... somehow.

Marcie gave a call from her room. Lillian pushed the covers back and slowly swung her legs over the side of the bed.

"Mama's coming, baby. Just a minute..."

It was painful for Lillian to stand up straight as she tied her bathrobe around her and shuffled, like an old woman, to her daughter's bed.

Marcie, who had been lying quietly in her crib, stood to greet her mother with arms stretched.

"Mama, mama, mama."

"Yes, darling, come to mama."

Lillian had a dull headache behind her eyes. Maybe she should just make a quick getaway now, pack a few things in a suitcase, get in her car and go as far as her thirty-eight dollars would get her. At least she wouldn't have to face Morris again.

She set the baby on the floor. Marcie ran to the window and craned her neck to look upwards through the branches. Lillian sat back into the rocker. She could hardly walk; how could she get away? What she really wanted was to visit Harold Winston today.

"Ouch!"

Lillian took a firm hold of Marcie under the armpits and lifted her off her leg as she tried to climb up, then cuddled her for a minute.

"Let's go warm you a bottle of milk, little one. At least we can start there."

At the stairs, Marcie turned to back down, step by step, on her hands and knees. Lillian went slowly with her, glad for the pace. She warmed a bottle on the stove, tested a drop against her wrist then handed it to Marcie, who sat astride her rocking horse, sucked her bottle into the air and rocked the horse with her hips.

Lillian lit a cigarette and leaned against the kitchen counter. It looked cold and rainy out, but she could still go for a car ride. That's what she would do… anything to get out of the house and think. After she finished her smoke, she gathered Marcie up in her arms, ignored her new companion *pain* the best she could, and climbed the stairs to get them dressed.

Lillian found some warm pants and a soft sweater for Marcie and, with great cunning and patience, found a way to get her clothes on her.

When she pulled off her own nightgown in front of the mirror, she wasn't surprised to find a large purple and black bruise the size of a hand, formed over the bone of her right hip. Lillian snorted. Her shin had a bruise, too, and a cut that never did bleed. It just really hurt whenever she walked.

No one had ever struck her before. Aside from the pain, she didn't like having to cower in fear of her life. For the moments that she had been on the floor with Morris over her, Lillian had felt a loss of her own dignity. Not a loss, exactly, but an absence. She had never questioned her own dignity before because she had never felt its presence... she just naturally had it. Everyone does.

But, when he hit her and held power over her like that, a fierce protection sprang up. Lillian refused to let him take away her dignity ever again. Something struck her deep in her core, and she knew that she *had* to leave this man.

She looked at her own naked body, so vulnerable and battered. Lillian decided to put on her warm, wool trousers and a cashmere sweater. She would drive to see Harold. He lived somewhere on the east side of town – she could surely find him.

Downstairs, she set Marcie on the floor, then went to get her keys from where they hung by the back door. When she reached for them, they weren't there. In two seconds she knew... he had taken them. He wasn't going to let her go anywhere! She looked around, flabbergasted, then heard Marcie push a chair across the floor and went to find her.

"Here, baby, let me help you."

Lillian swiped at tears. She reached onto the high shelf for the doll that Marcie was trying to get to. Inside, large chunks of herself broke off and fell away – plummeted. She sat and held the doll while it was examined carefully by her daughter, each texture fully realized under her small probing fingers.

The wind picked up outside. Lillian heard sharp raindrops cut against the window and she convulsed in a body shiver. She wanted to go back to bed, under the covers, where it was warm and safe, and never come out.

"Mama, mama, mama."

Marcie scrambled and climbed her way up her mother's thigh until she stood on her lap, then cupped her mother's crying face. Her own face was awash with love and concern for Lillian, her sad mama. Lillian set the doll down, wiped her face with her sleeve, then smooched up her baby.

"Let's call Florence, Marcie. She'll know what to do."

She swiftly set the child in her high chair, fixed her a piece of bread and butter with strawberry jam, then picked up the telephone.

"Hello, Lavonne. Hook me up with Florence Kaplan, please... Garden 4-3327."

"Yes ma'am. One moment please."

Lillian breathed into her closed fist. The house was cold this morning.

"I have Mrs. Kaplan on the line, Mrs. Scharf. Go ahead."

"Thanks, Lavonne."

"You're welcome, ma'am."

"Lillian, is that you?"

What a relief to hear her friend's voice. Lillian had to wait a moment for fear of crying.

"Hello? Lil, are you there?"

"Yes, I'm here. Hello, Flo. It's good to hear your voice."

She looked over toward Marcie who was happily oblivious to the jam ring that had formed all the way around her mouth.

"What's wrong, honey? You don't sound so good. What's going on?"

"Hold on a minute, Flo. I'll be right back."

Lillian set the receiver down on the shelf, then limped to the back door. Up on her tiptoes, she peered out the high window. There was no sign of Morris or his car anywhere. She shuffled back to the phone.

"Florence, I've got to get out of here. I don't want to talk about it on the telephone."

She rubbed the tender spot on the back of her leg.

"Please come get me – we'll go out."

"This sounds serious."

"It is. Believe me, it is. Come quickly. I want to get out of here before Morris comes back from basketball."

She examined a broken nail on her thumb; bit it off with the tips of her teeth.

"He's usually home by noon, so I only have another hour. Please hurry."

"Okay, honey. I'll be there in fifteen minutes. I need to get dressed."

"Thanks, Flo. I'll tell you everything."

Lillian was ready when Florence pulled up in her driveway. She threw the diaper bag in the back seat and climbed into the front with Marcie on her lap.

"Lil', what's...?"

Lillian turned toward her friend.

"Get me out of here... now. Drive toward East Park."

She gripped the armrest on the door – one arm firmly

around her baby.

As they drove away, the windshield wipers clacked back and forth. Florence glanced over at Lillian, whose eyes, normally so bright and lively, now looked troubled and severe. She sat close to the large steering wheel, hands at ten and two, leaned forward and peered into the dark day of wind and rain.

"You've been crying."

Lillian nodded a yes, but stared straight ahead. She didn't speak for a minute. Marcie, who had snuggled into a quiet ball, sucked her thumb and twirled a toggle button on her mother's coat.

"What's going on, Lil?"

In a flat quiet voice, Lillian answered.

"After I saw you yesterday, I went home. When I got there, Morris was angry."

The engine chugged rhythmically as they paused at a stop sign. There weren't many people out; it was too nasty and cold.

"What about?"

Lillian pulled Marcie's hood off, then smoothed her sweaty hair back from her face.

"My father called him and told him that I want to leave him."

A moment went by.

"Oy. This really *is* bad."

"He hit me, Flo. He smacked me in the head and I fell against the dresser and got a bad bruise on my hip and one on my shin. Then, he kicked me real hard, too, right in the back of my leg."

Her face contorted as she remembered.

Florence reached out for Lillian's hand.

Lillian spat her words.

"Then we went out for dinner where he told me I can't be in the play anymore and afterwards he had his usual non-participatory way with me and…"

She shrieked.

"… when I went to drive my car today, he had taken my keys so I can't go anywhere. I have to get out of there!"

Florence pretended there was something out the windshield that required her serious attention. What do you say to something like that? She looked over at Lillian whose eyes burned directly into hers. She whispered.

"Oh my, that's all so terrible… just terrible."

Lillian leaned her head back against the top of the seat.

"I need a cigarette."

"What are you going to do, Lil?"

They were just past the bridge on the other side of downtown. Florence pulled over under a stand of maples and stopped the car. The rain on the roof created a soft roar inside. Lillian cracked the window. Marcie had fallen asleep and lay curled on the bench seat between them. She dug a cigarette out of her coat pocket, lit it with her gold lighter, took a huge draft and finally blew a cloud of smoke toward the window. Most of it stayed in the car, but she didn't notice. Neither did Florence.

"And, that's not all."

"There's more?"

"Yeah. Someone burned a Star of David on our lawn last night…"

Florence gasped and covered her mouth with her hand. She looked at Lillian, who sat with her head back against the seat. Cigarette smoke twirled slowly upwards. Lillian turned her head toward Florence and locked eyes with her.

"I'm going to leave him, Flo. He's a brute and he thinks he owns me. Well..."

She flicked her ash into the ashtray.

"He doesn't own me. No one owns me but me, despite what *he* thinks."

Florence said nothing... she couldn't talk. She saw Lillian being spun and tumbled as though stirred in a large cauldron. So many problems... her life was such a mess right now. Florence thought of Sam and the quiet, easy life they shared together.

"The first thing I have to do is find Harold Winston. This whole thing is his fault..."

"Oh, Lil, you can't say that."

Lillian flapped her hand in the air.

"I know that, for heaven's sake. What if I had never, um, you know... with Harold? I would still be living my old life with Morris and wouldn't even know yet what an unbelievable creep he really is. How right my mother was."

She shifted her weight carefully onto her opposite hip.

"No, I'm grateful to Harold Winston. He's helping me begin to see something better than life as the wife of Mr. Scharf."

She paused, picked a bit of tobacco off her lip and flicked it away.

"Of course, it's all speculative at this point. I'm still

with Morris, and I don't know how to get out of there."

"Boy, I don't either."

"And...."

Lillian smashed the butt into the ashtray.

"I want to see Harold. I feel like I've lived twelve years since I saw him. Maybe he's... not who I remember he is."

She fell back against the car seat, deflated.

"Guten himmel, Florence, what have I done?"

Florence's face wore a mixture of compassion and incredulity.

"I know, I mean, I don't know. I don't know what to say."

For a few minutes they both sat – lost in thought – as the rain drummed quietly and continuously onto the car. Florence watched Lillian and worry rose up in her. What could she possibly do to help? Did she know someone who could help?

"Lil, is there anyone from the play who could tell you where Harold lives? What about Moody Luckle? That guy knows everyone."

"Hmmm...."

Lillian turned her head toward her side window which was completely fogged up. With her finger, she drew a heart and put her initials inside. Underneath, she added H.W. Then, she took a swipe with her palm and erased it.

"I don't want to see Moody today. He's way too cheerful."

Marcie roused – tried to get herself situated more comfortably. Lillian helped her turn over and tried, with great care, to keep her asleep longer. She looked at

Florence and held a finger to her lips. Both women sat perfectly still, barely breathed, while they watched the baby relax back down into her nap. What upheaval lay ahead for her little girl?

She spoke quietly.

"I can't think about how this will affect her. I have to trust that as long as she's with me, she'll be alright."

Florence bit her lower lip as a car hissed loudly past them on the road.

"You're really going to do this, aren't you?"

Lillian didn't answer because she didn't hear the question. She was going over every person in her mind she had seen at the rehearsal as she tried to link someone to Harold. Who would know where he lived? Stage manager... Al Flickenger? Lights, props, costumes... Millie!

"I know who can tell us... Millie Blovak. She lives on Glen Road, near the creamery. Turn right up here at the corner."

Florence jumped – her hands flew up to the wheel.

"Good, good. Let me start the car and we'll go."

She pulled out slowly onto the road and negotiated her way, with Lillian's help, through the neighborhood.

When they got there, Lillian took a hold of the door handle, then turned to Florence.

"I'll just run in and get the address from her. I'll be right back."

She eased her way out of the car so she wouldn't wake Marcie and stumbled in the rain up to the front door, then knocked rapidly five times with her knuckles as hard as she could. She looked down at her feet. Millie had to be home. She looked back at the car. Its wipers were going but she couldn't see in because of the rain.

The door creaked open and Lillian turned around.

"Well, hello there, Lillian. What a surprise! Come on in out of the rain."

Millie pulled the door open wider and stepped back. Lillian hopped quickly into the foyer. She smelled coffee and something delicious that had been baked recently.

"Hi, Millie. I'm... well, um... I'm...."

She wasn't sure what to say. She looked down. All around her feet were stacks of things: folded newspapers, rows of jars, a wooden box filled with dried plants. In the corner sat a treadle sewing machine with piles of cut cloth on the floor around it. Lillian saw the costume for Dorothy hanging on a nail in the wall. The play. She didn't get to be in the play. All the hope of a moment ago bled out of her as concern flooded through Millie.

"What is it, Lil? What's the matter?"

She ushered Lillian to a chair where she pulled off a stack of folded fabric and set it on the stairwell next to several other piles.

"Here, sit."

Lillian loosened the neck of her coat.

"Millie, some things have happened. Do you know where Harold Winston lives?"

In no hurry, Millie ambled her large body to a chair that sat beside her table, used the table for balance and eased her way down to it. She cocked her head to the side, pursed her lips and took a good perusal of Lillian.

"I do know where Harold lives. It's just a few blocks from here, on Rockland Road."

She looked directly at Lillian who tried to decide how much to tell her.

"My friend, Florence, brought me here."

She motioned back behind her, outside.

"My daughter's out there, too."

"Do you want them to come in?"

"No, no. I just need to talk to Harold..."

Millie's face questioned Lillian without words. She leaned forward, braced her elbows on her massive knees.

"Are you in some kind of trouble? To be perfectly honest, you don't look so good."

Immediately, Lillian's eyes filled with tears, but she checked herself.

"I'm... it's a long story, Millie. Things aren't great right now. I'd really like to see Harold Winston and Florence is out in the car..."

"Lillian, you're distraught. Do you want to tell me anything?"

"No. Harold will be able to help."

She hoped.

"He's... I'm..."

Millie smacked the tabletop with an open hand.

"Turn right at the corner, the way your car's facing. Go, um, three blocks, er, yeah, three. That'll be Rockland. Turn left. Harold lives second house in on the right... a stucco."

Lillian squinted.

"Right – three blocks, left – second on right. Right –

three blocks, left – second on right."

"Yes, but Lillian… listen to me."

Lillian repeated the directions over and over in her head while Millie talked to her.

"I can help you. Come to me if you need help. I will help you… whatever it is. Okay?"

Lillian turned her gaze toward Millie but, saw instead, a vision of herself flying gracefully off a cliff as a white bird with long, silky feathers.

"You come back here later, honey. I'll be here. I knew your mama, you know."

Those words brought Lillian back. She thanked Millie, hopped little steps of joy, then rushed forward and hugged her.

"I'll remember, Millie."

She blew her a kiss at the door then turned into the cold rain and ran stiff-legged to the car – repeated the directions to Harold's half out loud as she slithered into her seat.

16

Wind blew loud splatters of icy rain against the windshield.

"Right – three blocks, left – second on right."

Lillian winced in pain as she turned toward Florence.

"It's Harold's house. Let's go."

Marcie, who had obviously awakened, stood on Florence's lap with the huge steering wheel in her hands and smiled open-mouthed at her mother.

"Hi, Marcie baby."

The child turned back to her work and rolled the loose steering wheel from side to side. Florence, her hands around Marcie's waist, watched Lillian closely.

"How'd it go, Lil?"

"Let's go, Flo... really. Turn right up here, go three blocks, turn left on Rockland and he's the second house on the right."

She reached out for Marcie as Florence handed her over, but the child squirmed against the enforced end to her fun. She set up a wail, arched her back then slid down Lillian's lap nearly onto the floor of the car. The two women exchanged a look. This was not the time for this. Lillian struggled to reinstate Marcie onto her lap.

"Drive, Flo. Go up here and turn right... please."

The baby's cries, wails actually, kept conversation stopped and made the four block ride interminable for Florence. Lillian's attention was elsewhere. All she could see was Harold, standing across the room in the basement of the church, holding her hand as they wound their way through the sanctuary, his kind face and tender caresses....

Florence pulled up in front of a newer, small but well-kept stucco house on a street lined with young elm trees and new telephone poles. Lillian peered out the car window and wished he was standing there waiting for her. The only sign of life, though, that she could see through the rain, was a glow from a lamp in the front window.

Marcie's cries digressed into hiccups, then renewed into another round of full fledged screams. Lillian was torn. She wanted to bolt to the front door and leave the burden of her crying baby with Florence. She looked over at Flo, whose hands rested over the steering wheel and whose patient smile divulged nothing but compassion. No, if she really was going to leave Morris, she needed to get used to having her baby with her all the time. No more Clara, either. How would she ever survive?

"What do you want to do, honey?"

Florence, her sweet, sweet friend, had to shout over Marcie's noise.

Lillian used one arm to hold the child in her lap and tried to round up flailing little arms with the other, but was mostly unsuccessful.

"I'm going in. I'll take her with me. Hopefully he'll have something she can eat."

She glanced at the house.

"I hope he's home."

"Me, too. Here, let me carry her to the house for you."

"No, no… it's okay. I have to do it. Just wait until I'm inside, then you can go. I'll have Harold take me home… oh, no…"

She rolled her eyes.

"I'm going to have to go home later."

Lillian felt a huge drop inside herself, like a bad elevator ride. The enormity of what she was thinking of undertaking struck her. Was she really going to leave her husband… her whole life… her father… everyone she knew… everything she had?

"Lil, honey."

Florence laid her hand softly on her friend's cheek.

"You're going to be fine. You'll do fine. This is you we're talking about, Lil."

Lillian took a hold of her friend's hand then gave it a little kiss. In her breast; upheaval, interrupted by Marcie's shrieks. She was desperate to go.

"Well, whatever I do, they're going to say I'm crazy."

"Well, I know you're not. And, I won't betray you. I love you and will always be your friend, no matter...."

Florence broke down and cried, which made Lillian start, too. They tried to lean in toward each other to hug, but little screamer and flailer was between them. The two young women held hands tightly and looked lovingly into each other's watery eyes. Lillian mouthed the words bye-bye then reached over to the back seat for the diaper bag.

She opened the car door, ignored all pain, hoisted Marcie onto her left hip and limped her way through the rain to Harold's front door.

As Florence watched her best friend walk away, she dug a hanky out of her purse, wiped her eyes and blew her nose. After the door opened and Lillian went inside, she put the car in gear and drove home, sad and worried.

Harold had heard the car from his kitchen. The doorbell rang just as he walked toward the front window to see what was going on. He opened the front door to find Lillian, hair flattened and dripping wet, with her arms around a small, unhappy child who was perched on her hip. On her face Lillian wore a grimly determined look – mouth tight. But, when she saw Harold, she softened. Their eyes met and held.

"Come in, come in, Lillian. I'm so surprised to see you. What are you doing here?"

She couldn't talk or move. He hesitated, then his arm went around her shoulder to pull her in.

"What a nice surprise. I was just thinking about you.

And, who's this little marvel?"

He ushered them into his living room, fragrant with the smell of coffee.

Lillian bent over to set Marcie down, but the child would have none of it. She clung harder to her mother, which made the effort to stand up again twice as hard for Lillian. Harold watched with a glint of humor in his eye.

"This must be your very own daughter, then, eh?"

Marcie shook her head, pushed out her lower lip, grunted and turned away from Harold.

"Yes, Harold, this is Marcie, my daughter, who needs a new diaper and something to eat."

Lillian bounced the child to get a response, but Marcie's refusal was adamant.

"Can you stay awhile? Let's see what we have for her."

Harold walked toward the kitchen with his eyes glued to Lillian's. His eyebrows went up questioningly which prompted a flood of recent memories in her. She bit her lower lip and pleaded to him with her eyes. What was she pleading for?

In the kitchen, Harold opened the icebox. He pulled out a large, glass covered dish, took the cover off and held it up to Marcie. She flung her hand out and nearly knocked it to the floor.

"Say, Marcie! What's the matter with you?"

Lillian was embarrassed. Marcie had never behaved so badly before.

"Oh, it's alright. Don't worry about it."

The tone of his voice, the kind, sympathetic intimacy he conveyed to her... she believed him every time.

I'm a trusting fool. What am I doing here?

"I need to change her. Where should I go?"

Harold led them to a bedroom off the living room where Lillian spread out a small blanket on the bed. The whole time she changed Marcie she kept half her attention on Harold, who stood in the doorway with his hands in his pockets and looked really good. Neither one said anything. She held the dirty diaper away from her while she tried to figure out what to do with it so she could finish with Marcie. Harold stepped forward, took it and walked with it into the bathroom.

"I'll rinse this out, Lil."

Lillian couldn't believe it. Morris had never rinsed a diaper out... never.

Marcie lay placidly and looked around at the unfamiliar room. A small, framed photograph of a woman with a bustle and a parasol sat on the table next to the bed. Lillian leaned close in to see the woman's face, but she couldn't make it out very well. She could hear dishes clatter in the kitchen. Once she finished the diaper change, Marcie refused to walk. There was nothing for Lillian to do but hoist her up again.

Harold stood at the stove while he tended something in a sauce pan. Lillian smelled burnt match and coffee and was suddenly ravenous. He turned to her with a hungry look in his own eyes.

"Harold, I'm... I've come... there's..."

She gave up.

"I needed to see you."

He stirred slowly and spoke with a quiet voice.

"I'm happy to see you, Lil. You have no idea."

His eyes bore into hers. A wavelike shudder traveled through her.

"What brings you out on such a dreadful day? Would you like a cup of coffee?"

She could only nod yes. He was happy to see her. A small pinpoint of hope took up residence in her breast. Marcie reached for a spoon and lurched suddenly toward the table where a half drunk cup of coffee and a book lay. Lillian's balance was thrown off. She took a big step to keep a hold of her baby and landed up against the table. Harold dropped his spoon and scooped her into his arms. For a moment, they stood together – savored the closeness.

Marcie wriggled out of her mother's embrace and toddled around the kitchen. She pulled open a low cupboard, found some pots and pans and pulled them noisily out. Lillian raised an eyebrow at Harold.

"It's perfectly alright. It's good she's busy."

He leaned down and kissed her gently on her mouth.

"I'm so glad to see you, Lil. What's brought you here?"

The tenderness in his voice was too much for her. She rested her head against his chest as large tears spilled onto her cheeks. It took several minutes to gather herself together enough to be able to talk. Harold reached into his back pocket and pulled out his handkerchief. He carefully wiped her eyes and face.

"I'm crying a lot lately."

He helped her into a chair at the table and served her a small bowl of barley soup. Then, he sat in his regular place next to the stove, and caressed Lillian's hand under the table. Marcie came over, climbed onto her lap and ate bite after bite of the comforting food. Lillian took a couple of spoonfuls. As she ate, she relaxed. And, as she relaxed, a great fatigue came over her. All her troubles seemed far away, in a different life.

"Thank you for the delicious food, Harold. And, thanks for being home this afternoon."

Harold's smile was sunshine to Lillian.

"Well, I'm always around on Sundays. On a nice day, I might go for a walk or a drive, but I was thinking I'd just stay in today. It's miserable out."

"Yeah, well... my whole life's miserable right now. Never mind the stock market, *my* life is crashing."

Her head felt like lead.

"Why don't you come lie down on my davenport? You look beat."

They moved to the living room and took an assortment of pots and pans and other interesting kitchen implements with them. While Marcie sat and played on the rug with a nest of gadgets around her, Harold sat on the floor next to the davenport, where Lillian was curled under the afghan. His hand ran slowly up and down her arm, over her forehead, across her shoulder and softly over her rump.

"What's wrong, my lovely Lillian? What's happened to you?"

"I'm leaving Morris, that's what."

The words came out deflated. She had no more fight in her.

"He hit me. He told me I can't be in the play. He took my car keys. I hate him. I'm leaving him."

She closed her eyes, but a tear squeezed out and ran halfway down her cheek. Harold wiped it away, then held her hand in both of his and kissed each bent knuckle. He didn't say anything.

Lillian looked over at Marcie who didn't appear to listen. How much did a fourteen month old understand? Would she remember this?

"I'm trying to figure out how to leave Morris. I have thirty-eight dollars and four diapers. I have exactly one change of clothes for Marcie and none for me."

She was up on one elbow.

"If I'm going to leave him, I'm going to have to go back home, and I don't want to. I never want to see him again."

She flopped back onto the pillow and looked off with a frown.

As Harold stroked her arm, over and over, a quiet peacefulness entered the room. Lillian could hear the rain, but it sounded muffled and far away. The baby rolled onto her side and tried to put her feet against the rolling pin as she held on to it. Lillian's breathing slowed.

"I'm so glad you're here, Harold... I...."

He leaned forward and kissed her softly.

"You can stay here, Lil. There's room for both of you."

There it was... just the fantasy that Lillian had dreamed about. She could live with Harold and Marcie and do the play. They could move into that little bedroom and....

"Yeah, Morris would stand for that for about two seconds. It just wouldn't work, Harold. He'd come over here and physically drag me back. And, you know what?"

She snorted.

"He'd probably do it, too."

He looked longingly at her.

"We could hide you. You could stay in the house forever and I'll get you what you need. You'll never have to go out."

She tried to muster a smile.

"Oh, fun, Harold."

He whispered, looked sideways at Marcie.

"He hit you? He... *hit* you?"

He met her eyes and wouldn't let go. Lillian's darted around. The way Harold said it made it seem like an impossible thing... like that kind of thing had never occurred to him; the blow to her temple, the fall against the dresser, the way she slumped to the floor.

"Lillian? Lil? Look at me."

He caressed her cheek and gently turned her head toward him.

"Are you badly hurt... physically, I mean?"

"What's bad? Is a bruise the size of my hand, bad? Maybe it's not that bad. Maybe the bruise on the back of my leg doesn't matter either."

She scooted herself up into a sitting position, her voice went up a few notches.

"No, I'm not hurt that badly, Harold. I'm just fine. He's my husband, right? He can hit me if he wants to!"

She waved her hand, shooed him away.

"I'm just a lowly woman to him. He doesn't know I'm real. Well, surprise, Morris, I'm real. I'm real, too."

Her bottom lip trembled, she bit down hard.

Harold watched her, amazed.

"I won't live in that life anymore. I won't. Why would I stay with him when I know there are people like you in the world?"

She gathered her knees up in her arms and rested her forehead on them. After a minute, she turned her face toward Harold. He was the kindest man she had ever met, and the handsomest. Her body ached – it hurt. And the look on his face made her want to dive into his soul and rest there, forever.

A crash... shattered porcelain. They turned together. Marcie sat on the floor next to a pile of broken lamp, stunned. She held the electrical cord in her hand, eyes huge with fright. In a moment, she laid her head back and wailed as Lillian climbed off the couch and picked her up. She walked quickly around the room – patted Marcie's back.

"Shhh, it's okay. Shhh, now. Everything's alright. Mama's here."

Harold came into the room with a whisk broom in one hand and a dustpan in the other, then knelt to clean up the mess. Lillian stood with Marcie and watched. Inside her, a huge curve of darkness swooped down. This wasn't the right place to be. As attracted as she was to Harold, as kind and sweet as he was, she couldn't stay with him. Nothing about it felt right to her, except maybe for the idea of lying naked with him again. She nuzzled her baby's neck and walked to the front window.

Rain blew across the street in sweeping folds. If hope still lived in her, it had crawled under and behind, to sleep. Before her – no light... only a dark, threatening abyss –

nowhere to go, no one to turn to. She could not return to Morris. She couldn't.

Harold walked up behind her and encircled mother and child in his arms. He rested his chin on the top of Lillian's head.

"I can't give you the shelter you need, Lil. I can't protect you the way I would like to."

He pulled them up against himself. They watched tree limbs bend and sway in the wind.

"I do have something for you, though, my beauty."

Lillian barely heard his words. She breathed in the smell of him, the warmth of his closeness. He leaned around, kissed her cheek, her nose, her forehead, her mouth. Marcie lay, relaxed, in her mother's arms. Lillian savored every moment, every touch, every caress. After they kissed, her face remained upward – longed for more.

Harold stepped away, into his bedroom. A moment later he returned, slipped a wad of something into her hand and closed her fingers around it. Lillian looked down... money.

She made her way to a chair and sat as Marcie climbed down to pick up a spatula. She looked up at Harold.

"I didn't know a person could have this many tears."

Half laughing, half crying, she wiped her nose with her sleeve and counted the bills... two hundred and fifty dollars. She hung her head, shook it slowly in disbelief. Harold petted her hair, over and over. The wind blew, the clock ticked. From the bedroom, a faint chime sounded three times.

"I'll take you anywhere you want to go, Lil. Shall we put you on a train for somewhere?"

He sat down on the davenport, faced her and took her hand.

Lillian's head hurt. She barely had enough energy to sit up.

"I don't think I can do that right now, Harold. I'm just not ready."

She sat back and closed her eyes. She saw a bird with long, white feathers fly away from her, into darkness, and watched it until it disappeared into a speck. It was the same bird vision she had seen at Millie's. Millie. She would go see Millie. Without lifting her head, she spoke.

"Harold, you have given me so much. You've opened the whole world to me... and I'm not talking about the money."

She turned her head to look at him.

"I can never thank you enough."

A wan smile coaxed itself out of her.

It was Harold's turn to falter. His voice wavered.

"You are so beautiful, Lil. I don't want this to be over between us. We've barely begun to know each other."

His thumb ran around and over Lillian's hand.

"I have to do what I have to do, first, Harold."

"I know. I know."

He looked off, out the window. He didn't know what else to say, and couldn't say it, anyway, for the lump in his throat.

"Harold?"

"Yes, my dearest?"

"Will you drive us to Millie's? I think I'd better go there. Maybe she'll know what I should do."

He looked at the beautiful, beaten down young woman stretched out like a banana peel on his living room chair. He would take her to the moon, if he could. He wanted to tell her that he loved her, that he would go to the ends of the earth for her.

"Of course, my love. I'll drive you to Millie's. Let me gather your things."

Lillian found a cigarette in the pocket of her coat and lit it. She'd never been this far down. She was a slithering, scuttling, echoing, complete... no one – lightning around the edges... a lonely place. Her brain rattled in her head.

"Lillian, Lil...."

Harold shook her shoulder and Lillian opened her eyes. Luckily, she still held her cigarette and Marcie was right beside her. Harold took her under the arm, helped her up. Did she really have to leave Harold, too? Wasn't one wrenching in a day enough?

"Marcie, honey. Bring me your coat so we can go."
The little girl retrieved her jacket from the bench by the door. Lillian knelt down to help her put it on.

"What a smart girl you are, Marcie."

She had to keep herself going, for her daughter, at least.

"Let's go see Millie. She'll know what to do, I hope."

Lillian stood, put her coat on and faced Harold. He came close to her to kiss her, but she reached around his neck to hug him instead, then whispered in his ear.

"I'm a lost little lamb, Harold. I need to figure some things out. We might be able to be together some day... just not now."

She kissed him delicately on the lips. Then, with no

more thought to her physical discomfort, she scooped Marcie up and followed Harold to his car.

17

Morris paused in bewilderment on the landing half way down the stairs. Where was Lillian? She should be home. He checked the little table under the stairs next to the phone for a note, but found nothing. Except for a mess of crumbs and jam on Marcie's tray, the kitchen appeared tidy and unused. He pulled and stretched the sleeves of his sweater over his wrists, then smoothed his hair back. They weren't upstairs. They weren't in the house and her car was still in the garage. He looked out the window of the landing. What a lousy day... cold, rainy, windy. She certainly wasn't out walking the baby.

Downstairs, he flipped the radio on to hear the

monotone voice of Randall Arch.

"... song to hit the airwaves. See how this new release, destined to be a classic, sits in the belly of your latest woes... 'Happy days are here again, the skies above are clear again, so let's sing a song of cheer...'"

Morris abruptly switched the radio off then stood, frowned and looked out the front window at his blackened front yard. His molars ground loudly against each other. He had heard from a couple of the fellows, Harry Cohen and Ben Levinson, when their own lawns had been doused with gasoline and they, too, had been publicly branded as dirty Jews, for all to see. The men of the Scharf family prided themselves on their level of assimilation and their ability to get along in the business community.

Reuben Scharf, Morris' father, had brought twelve Jewish merchants into Mason City, sponsored the men; offered loans, with interest, to help them get started. Many came from New York City after emigrating from Russia. They sent for their wives and young children only when they had accumulated enough wealth to support them in reasonable style. Over twenty-five years, the men had established themselves as dependable, hardworking members of the town.

Last night's transgression of his private property left a ragged sore in Morris' stomach. He remembered his grandmother's awful stories of how the Cossacks burned their village back in Russia... everything lost. Surely Mason City, Iowa, was a more civilized place.

As Morris leaned a hand on the window frame, his mind alternated between his yard and his wife. He couldn't even think about the economy right now. Rain, driven by gusty wind, splattered heavily against the window. He thought he heard something in the kitchen and listened sharply, but, no.

It was lunch time. Lillian hadn't even fixed him something to eat. He swallowed down a large lump of emotion and went into the kitchen, paced from the hallway to the breakfast nook and back again several times, then stopped in front of the icebox and cranked it open. There, on the shelf, wrapped in white butcher paper, sat the steaks for their Sunday dinner.

Morris stood up straight, slammed the door shut, shoved his hands in his pockets. Where was she? This was unacceptable. He must find her and bring her home. In a city of twenty-three thousand people, though, he didn't know where to begin to look.

He suddenly tore up the stairs, threw open the door to the cedar closet and searched madly about. Despite the chill in the small room, he wiped sweat from his forehead with his sleeve. He stopped when he found what he was looking for: her suitcase. She was just out... nothing to worry about.

Morris went back into the hall, closed the closet door behind him and palmed his hair back off his face. His heart thudded against his backbone. He turned to the right, paced toward his bedroom then turned and paced back down the hall. The edges of his mouth worked and his hands gesticulated.

The best thing to do at a time like this was go to his mother's. If he didn't feel better there, and he was sure to find some comfort amid the old clutter and familiar fixtures of his childhood home, at least his mother would fix him lunch.

Morris took a couple of deep breaths and continued on down the stairs. His shoulders released a little and there was almost a spring in his step. He didn't want to stay in the house for another moment. The question of where Lillian *was* curled around in the back of his mind as he hucked his long rain coat on and pulled the door shut behind him.

Head down, braced into the wind and rain, he hurried down the driveway and jumped into his car. There were few people on the road, so the drive to his mother's home took four minutes.

He let himself in the front door and was immediately hit with the scent of fried onions. His mouth watered. Never mind Lillian for the moment – never mind the economy or the burnt spot on his lawn. He was home again, where the small boy inside of his large body welled up and overtook him. He walked toward the kitchen at the back of the house.

"Mother? It smells awfully good in here."

From the pantry, Morris heard a cupboard door close. As he reached the kitchen, a short, round woman in a faded flowered apron waddled in. Her hair was bound in an old kerchief and little clumps of white hairs sprang out from beneath the edges around her face. Cecil Scharf was no beauty, but her face lit up when she saw her firstborn son. She threw her hands up.

"Bubbela. My Morrishka. It's so good to see you."

She pointed to the table. "Here, sit down, have something to eat. Then tell me about your daughter and that German wife of yours."

As she talked, she went to the stove and stirred something in the pan. Then she took a plate down and served Morris a large, steamy helping of salty dumplings with onions and cracklings. He was in heaven. Lillian's food never tasted as good as this. The smells of his mother's kitchen, the savory food before him, the rain against the windows… Morris was a lucky man.

"What is this business with the banks? Your brother says we don't have to worry, but it sounds bad to me. What do you think, Morris?"

Morris couldn't talk with his mouth stuffed as it was. He shook his head.

"No? No problem? Is that what you're saying?"

He nodded yes then took a drink of water.

"It's not so bad. You don't have to worry about anything, Mother. I will take care of you. You know that."

He could hardly stop eating long enough to talk.

Cecil, with wooden spoon still in hand, stood beside Morris, hands on hips and watched his every bite.

"Is good, no? Your father, he liked this. How is my little Marcela? Bring her over, Morrishka; I want to see her again. Your brother Abe, what a schlemiel… he's gone and put a dent in his car. I have a light bulb out over the back door…."

She waved her wooden spoon around like a mad conductor; pointed to things, emphasized with a smack into her palm.

As he ate, Morris tuned his mother out and thought about Lillian. This economic downturn, the burning on their lawn... she ought to be home. Things were too unstable in the world for a woman to be out on a day like this. Why, she should be home to make Sunday dinner. Where was she?

Suddenly, it was difficult to swallow. Morris loosened the button at his neck and stretched his chin up and around to make more room for his large Adam's apple.

Cecil sat stiffly in the chair next to him. Her knees spread apart a little which pulled the hem of her dress tight across them. He caught a glimpse of her stockings rolled down to her knees and looked away, disgusted.

"Oy, Morris. My back hurts so much every day. I can hardly walk anymore."

She winced and looked off.

"I don't know what I'm going to do... How'm I going to walk up the stairs?"

Morris knew exactly what to say to her as she asked him the same questions and told him the same stories every time he went to visit her.

"Don't worry about it, Mother. You're going to be just fine."

He looked at his old mother. All she did was complain. It's all she had ever done. His father, Reuben, knew how to handle her, though.

Young Morris chewed his beef as his parents argued at the table. They spoke Russian, which he could understand when he wanted to. Today they fought about whether or not they should invite his father's cousin, Anna Lipka, to his Bar Mitzvah. He wiped a ring of grease from around his mouth with his napkin and watched the veins in his father's leonine forehead stand out farther and farther.

"You invite her, that's all. She's family."

Reuben Scharf pounded his hand on the table. The dishes rattled.

Cecil wouldn't back down. She couldn't stand his cousin, with her loose, careless ways.

"She's a floozy and you know it."

"She's my cousin!"

"I don't want that slut at my son's Bar Mitzvah. She'll parade her bosom around for all the men to drool over. It's not appropriate for my Morris."

She grabbed the broom, elbows high, and swept out from under the table as the two younger sons lifted their feet to keep out of her furious way.

"By the time we are celebrating, after the service, Morris will be a man. It's good. He should see a woman's bosoms. That's what they're for."

Reuben leaned across the corner of the table and cupped his fourteen year old daughter's newly budded breast through her blouse, then gave it a quick jiggle under his hand. Sonia's eyes got big and round and she held her fork motionless in mid-air.

Morris read the look on his sister's face. Something was going on in her, some big emotion. Her eyeballs suddenly floated in unshed tears. His mother was bent down to see under the table. That's when he looked at his father. Reuben pulled his hand off his daughter like it was scorched.

"He's nearly a man."

He wiped his mouth and hands with his napkin, pushed his chair back. As he stood, he pounded the table once more with both hands. His voice took on a deep, authoritative tone.

"She'll come, wife. That's the end of it."

He looked directly at Morris, winked, then retreated to the living room to read his paper.

Cecil hadn't seen what Morris had seen. She swept, with her eyes on her work, and continued to complain, even when Reuben had left the room.

She spoke under her breath.

"I'm tired of that woman's brazenness. She doesn't know a thing about raising children or keeping a nice house. All she does is flit from one man to the next, flaunting her..."

"Enough, woman!"

Reuben appeared in the doorway, jaw set. The four children turned their heads in unison to look at him when he spoke. Cecil stopped her sweeping.

"I said she'll come and I mean it. Invite her to the reception. Anna Lipka will come as our guest to celebrate our son's Bar Mitzvah. That's the end."

He slapped the folded newspaper against his thigh and raised his voice.

"I don't want to hear about it again!"

Then he turned and went back to the living room.

The menacing edge in his father's voice excited Morris. He looked at his sister with her head bowed at the table.

Yes, a man was a good thing to be, especially compared to being a girl. Morris sat up straighter and dug into the rest of his roast.

In his mother's kitchen, with his belly full, Morris wondered what to do next. He didn't want to tell her about Lillian's absence. The news of that would travel through the ladies' grapevine like a blotter. But, where was she? And, how could he find her?

"... Isn't that true, Morrishka? Don't you think so?"

Morris waved his mother off with one hand.

"Yes, yes, of course it's true. That's right."

He didn't know what she had said, but with her, it didn't matter anyway. He wiped his mouth and hands with his napkin, then stood.

"How about the paper? Why don't I sit and read the paper here for a while?"

Cecil's homely face lit up from the inside.

"Oh, what a good idea. Here, Morris. Sit in your father's chair."

Her hands clasped together over her breast in happiness. Seldom did her firstborn son stay for a visit past having a meal. She hobbled over to the coffee table where she picked up the paper and handed it to Morris.

"Here, my son, make yourself comfortable."

She fluffed a pillow on the big, overstuffed chair just as Morris sat down. Then she walked back to the kitchen doorway, turned, wiped her hands on her apron and stood and proudly watched her handsome son read the newspaper.

Morris couldn't read a word – but he pretended to – in order to gain a little time. Someone must know where Lillian was. She had to be with someone. He tried to think of the people Lillian knew, but could only picture a vast, empty space. Who was that woman she was always chattering on about? It was Sam Kaplan's wife. But, what was her name? Fanny? Florence? Yes, that was it – Florence.

He threw the paper down, rose out of his chair, smoothed his hair back and grabbed his coat. In an instant he had kissed his mother on the cheek and left. She stoically returned his stingy embrace. Then, he forged ahead against the wind and rain and ran to his car.

He'd already driven half a block before he realized he didn't know where he was going. Morris pulled the car over and stopped. He needed to go to the Kaplan's. Why was he heading north? He opened the door and stepped out into the rain onto a slippery mat of wet leaves, caught a hold of himself, then looked up. And, just as quickly, he backed into the car, pulled his legs in and closed the door.

He sat, baffled, and wiped his face with his wet sleeve. Rain thrummed, the car's motor pulsed. Morris tried to latch onto a thought, but all thoughts swirled and dodged him. Lillian's face flickered, loomed close, changed shape. A large burnt spot on his lawn... that fat, stupid policeman. No money... no one buying new furniture, beds... Lillian's face... Lillian!

He shook his head and cracked the window. Then he looked in the rearview mirror, smoothed his hair back, pulled the car around and drove in the opposite direction, toward Florence's house.

He would tell her that she needed to come home, immediately. The front lawn needed tending to and it was nearly time to start dinner in order for it to be ready by 5:30.

At the front door he rapped sharply a couple of times and bent over to peer in through the small window. He saw Sam Kaplan walk toward the door from the back of the house in his bathrobe. Sam was not in the crowd of fellows that Morris normally did business with, but, at shul, he counted as one of ten men in a minyan. The fact that he was Jewish gave Morris confidence... they spoke the same language. God was above man and man was above woman. Morris shivered as the rain blew under the brim of his hat, down the back of his neck. He had a few things to say to his wife and he intended to say them.

The moment the door opened, Morris stepped inside. He pulled his hat off and batted it against his thigh to get the water off. From the living room, he heard a man's voice talk rapidly on the radio.

"Hello, Morris."

Sam, normally calm and easygoing, was no different this afternoon. His voice sounded like he had seen Morris five minutes before – like he expected him.

Morris dripped where he stood. His eyes traveled around the entryway, up the stairs, through the doorways that led to other rooms in the house, and down the hall to the kitchen.

"Yes, hello Sam. I'm looking for Lillian. I have reason to believe she's here."

Sam slowly shut the front door with a pensive look on his face.

"No sir."

He looked Morris in the eye.

"She's not here."

Their gaze held for a moment, then Morris narrowed his eyes.

"She's not here?"

"No. She's not here."

"Well, where is she?"

He fingered the wide brim of his fur felt hat. That tremble was back in his stomach. Some of his lunch churned and then lurched, and a bit of bile rose. The taste of burnt onion stung back down behind his nostrils. Morris cleared his throat.

Sam motioned to the living room.

"Would you like to come in, Morris? I can get you..."

"No!"

His voice rang loudly. He lowered it.

"Where is she... my wife?"

He stood up straight and looked suspiciously around, as though she might be hiding around the corner, in one of the rooms.

Florence, like an apparition, stood quietly in the kitchen way, wrapped in her sweater. She had her collar clenched in a fist at her neck. At the cold look on her face, Morris reeled back a step, stuck his hand out against the wall and caught himself.

Florence took a few steps toward him. Her words were flat, just this side of hostile.

"She's not here."

Morris shot a look at Sam, whose neutral face gave away nothing. He cleared his throat again, stood up straight and spoke in a deep, hopefully calm, voice.

"Will you tell me where she is? Do you *know* where she is?"

"No."

"No, what? No, you don't know where she is, or no, you won't tell me?"

Florence moved over next to her husband and he put his arm around her shoulder. She spoke quietly, carefully.

"My only answer for you today, Morris, is no. My answer is no."

Morris sputtered, anger spilled out.

"What do you mean you won't...?"

Sam firmly braced two hands up and faced Morris, like a cop. Morris stopped in mid-question.

"Morris, your wife's not here."

He lowered his hands, turned to Florence.

"Do you know where she is?"

Florence shook her head. No, if she were perfectly honest. She might still be with Harold, or she might be on her way to the moon. This was Lillian they were talking about, and there was no telling what she might be up to.

"You don't know where she is? Is that what you're saying?"

Florence nodded once, then no one said anything for several seconds. Benny Goodman's sweet clarinet called to them from the radio and Morris cleared his throat again.

"Did you see her this morning?"

Florence's affirmative nod was barely discernible. She hugged herself and leaned in closer to Sam.

Morris was nearly out of patience.

"You saw her this morning? And you don't..."

"Morris. Listen."

Sam put his hand on the other man's shoulder.

"Listen. Florence drove Lillian somewhere this morning. She..."

"What? You drove her somewhere? Where?"

He wanted to lash out at the stupid woman, but he used a modicum of restraint. He could when he had to.

Florence had the fingers of her fist pushed against her set mouth. She said nothing, but slowly and deliberately shook her head no.

A volcano of anger nearly erupted out of Morris. This was ridiculous. He lowered his voice.

"Tell me where Lillian is. Tell me! Where is she?"

Sam Kaplan had never seen Morris Scharf in such a state. He didn't know what had transpired between the women, only that Florence had returned home several hours earlier with red-rimmed eyes and a determination, despite his questions, not to say anything to him about Lillian.

"Listen, Scharf. You're not going to threaten my wife here this afternoon. I think it would be best if you were on your way. She doesn't know anything, and, if she does, it's obvious that she's not going to tell anyone."

"She has to tell me. I'm the husband... I have a right to know."

Morris stood up tall, shook water off his coat and hiked

it up onto his shoulders. He towered over Florence and Sam. Such little people, such little minds, such little lives. There was nothing more to say. He opened the front door, and, with a minute nod of civility, turned and left.

Rain pelted him on his way to the car. He made a quick dive into the driver's seat, slammed the door shut and sat there. Damnation. She took her somewhere. Where? Where, in this town, would Lillian want to go on a Sunday morning? And, why wouldn't that woman tell him where she took her? It was *his* wife they were talking about... his! He slammed both fists onto the steering wheel.

Why did Lillian have to be so difficult? He had their lives perfectly ordered. Morris started his car. If she would just behave in a more wifely fashion, they could get through this... economic trouble. She was messing everything up right at the time she should be standing by his side. So where was she? He brooded as he drove home through the darkened, rainy streets.

As he neared his house on the newly developed and highly sought after, Woodshire Drive, it occurred to Morris that Lillian had probably returned there. It was the sensible thing to do on a gloomy day. He sat up straighter. Yes, Lillian was sensible, normally. That's why he married her... that, and her looks. There weren't any other women in town who were as good looking as Lillian Scharf, even among the goys. It gave Morris a strong sense of pride when he walked around town or did business, to think that his own wife was better looking than everyone else's. He not only had the best looking wife, he also had a new house, one of the largest in Mason City. All things considered, there was absolutely no reason for her to leave him.

He pulled up in the driveway and parked directly in front of the garage door. He paid no attention to his desecrated front yard as he strode confidently in.

"Lillian? I'm home."

Not a sound. He walked through to the kitchen. Crumbs still sat untouched on the high chair tray. In the living room, only the sound of the clock and the rain splatter against the windows broke the stillness and silence. Morris checked the clock... 1:20. He paced in a circle, ground his teeth furiously, smoothed his hair back several times. Nothing was right. He didn't know what to do.

He was seven. Ever since his birthday last week, Morris was allowed to walk all the way around the block by himself. So, today he was going to do it for the first time. He started out and skipped toward the corner past Mrs. Friesner's house with a cat in the window, then the garden that old Mr. Alcorn was always working in, then the Blatt's and their mean barking dog – good thing it was tied up.

When he reached the corner he slowed to a cautious walk. He had been around the block before with his father. They liked to take walks on Shabbas. But, Morris had never ventured out on his own like this before. He pulled some bravery into his chest and stepped carefully over the crack in the sidewalk. It wasn't so bad. He began to look around at the houses and trees. His arms swung by his side. The sun warmed his back through his light jacket.

Across the street, Morris saw some big kids playing in

an open garage. He stopped to watch. After a few minutes, one of them noticed him standing there and motioned to him to come over. Morris shook his head no, so the boy walked across the street toward him.

"Come over. We'll play a game."

"I'm not supposed to."

The boy looked at Morris like he was trying to figure something out.

"Come on. Just come over."

The way he said it made Morris feel alright about going. He wasn't a mean boy.

They crossed the street together. Morris came up to the other boy's armpits.

They walked up the driveway into the garage. Another child, a girl, placed a tire on top of a pile of tires that was as high as her chest. She looked at the boy, then grabbed Morris by the arm and jerked him behind the stack of tires with his arms held back. The big boy squatted and yanked down Morris's pants and underpants to his ankles. They took turns spanking him hard on his butt, then the big girl flopped his penis a few times. Neither one spoke, but they worked furiously, like a team.

Snot poured from Morris's nose, but he couldn't wipe it. He cried, but they told him to shut up. He wanted his mama so bad.

They lifted him by the arms and lowered him into the middle of the stacked up tires.

"Shut up or we'll tell your parents what a little sissy you are. You're pathetic. You'd better stay here for an hour or we're going to tell."

He heard their footsteps as they ran away, then he tipped his head forward and threw up into his own little hands. Morris sank down into a hopeless, wretched pit.

In his living room, Morris pushed his fists into his temples and gave out a moan. He hated that girl. He could remember her voice and how terrible he felt when she...

He spun around and stumbled toward the liquor cupboard. He poured a fast shot of Scotch and downed it in one swallow. He poured another and threw it down his throat, then stood with hands on thighs while his seared insides burned away his memories.

When he eventually stood up, Morris was wobbly, but ready for action. He slammed his fist into his other palm like a catcher's mitt.

18

Harold pulled the car up in front of Millie's house and parked. Lillian was anxious to go in, but when she turned toward him to say goodbye, a huge bubble of destiny pressed against her so hard that she could barely breathe. Maybe her true fate was to be with Harold and now she was about to make the wrong fate happen for herself.

Marcie stood on the seat between them with her arms spread across the seat back. Lillian kept an eye on her daughter – where she stepped, how she balanced.

"Harold… I want to tell you that we'll be together. I want us to be. I just don't know... I don't know anything except that I have to go in and see Millie."

Tears waited... poised to spill.

Marcie stepped on Harold's lap and took a hold of the big steering wheel. He put his hands around her waist to steady her. The wipers flew back and forth – afforded a split second of clarity through the windshield before the rain filled in. Lillian saw Millie's porch light on even though it was afternoon. She had noticed the clock just as they left Harold's... ten minutes after three. His lower lip trembled as Harold held the little girl.

"Lillian... Lil."

He turned his head and looked into her eyes.

They're hazel, Lillian thought. And they're beautiful and I'd better get out of here or else I'm not going to make it. She scooted across the seat and threw her arms around his neck. He held the baby and she held him – whispered in his ear.

"Thank you, Harold. I'll write to you. Thank you for the money... for everything. You've given me more than you know, but I've got to go now."

She got out of the car, grabbed the diaper bag then ran around to the driver's side. Harold opened the door and handed her daughter over. A sharp pain ran down her leg as she hoisted the child onto her hip, and her heart bound itself into a tight knot.

He stood, drenched, beside his car as he watched her limp away up the walk. She banged the knocker twice then turned and threw him a kiss. He was still there when Millie opened the door and pulled them inside.

Lillian cried rivulets of tears, which added to her overall wetness. She pulled Marcie's hood off and brushed the child's hair back off her face – tried to get control of her emotional state.

Millie put her solid arm around Lillian's shoulders.

"What a day you're having, huh? Here, let me take her."

Lillian could only manage a nod.

She was sent to the bathroom to take a hot bath while Millie undid Marcie. As she eased herself down into the steaming water, the relief Lillian felt brought up more tears. She gently scooped bath water over her face, then she lay with her head on the back rim of the claw foot tub.

The bruise on her hip was dark purple with yellow edges. It felt like the bone underneath it was cracked or chipped, it was so painful to the touch. She ran both hands lightly up and over her breasts and down her stomach, then around under her thighs and back over the tops again. Images flew through her brain like shooting stars: Harold kissing her, Morris's angry face over her, her father's bulging eyes, sweet Florence, crying. Was she completely selfish? What was she doing? Before she succumbed to the onslaught of bad thoughts, Lillian slipped under the water with only her nose left above. The muffled quiet and hot water relaxed and transported her. Millie would help her. She already was.

Wrapped warmly in a big terry cloth bathrobe, a towel on her head, Lillian joined Millie and Marcie in the cluttered kitchen where the inviting smell of something savory kindled a speck of happiness inside her. A space on the table was cleared in front of where Marcie sat and demolished a muffin. A pile of crumbs grew under her busy fingers.

"Here, Lillian, sit here."

As Millie cleared away piles of newspapers, Lillian noticed a stack of Best Detective magazines on a stool near the stove.

"You read detective stories, Millie?"

"I sure do. I like figuring things out. It's a challenge for me to see if I can tell who done it before it's given away in the story."

Lillian nodded weakly and looked at the mess in front of Marcie.

"Can you tell me how my story is going to end? Where am I going to end up?"

"Well, dearie, let's find out, eh? What's going on? Tell me what's wrong."

As they talked, Millie slowly moved from stove to shelves to table and back. She cooked, put things away, moved things around: plates, piles of papers and fabrics of astounding colors and textures. The dress for Dorothy hung next to the sewing machine in the corner. The play... the scarecrow... another loss for Lillian. A band tightened around her head.

"What's wrong? Ha. What's right's more like it."

Millie put a strong hand on Lillian's shoulder and gave her a reassuring squeeze.

"Things aren't too good at home?"

Lillian shot her a sideways look.

"I don't ever want to go home."

Marcie looked up at her mother questioningly, her sticky fingers covered with crumbs. Lillian quickly rose, gathered the small hands in hers and rolled them clean with her fingers. Marcie reached up to be picked up.

"Mama…."

"Don't worry, baby. You're staying with me."

Lillian hugged Marcie as she sat back down at the table. Then she fed her small bites of the muffin and the child calmed down.

With some effort, Millie leaned over, braced a hand on one knee and, with hot pad in hand, pulled a pie out of the oven, then set it on the stove. She was out of breath.

"Here, we'll let this cool a bit. Now, you said you don't want to go home. Tell me why not."

"It all feels wrong there. My whole life is wrong."

"Your whole life?"

Millie pulled a chair away from the table and laboriously sat.

"I want a different life, Millie. I don't want to stay with Morris. I can't stand him anymore."

She chewed the inside of her cheek.

"I'm scared of him."

"What'd he do?"

"Well, what he did is almost beside the point. It's who he is, what he believes."

Millie cocked an eyebrow.

"What did he do?"

Lillian gnawed the inside of her cheek harder and furiously rubbed the hair back off Marcie's forehead over and over until the child squawked, arched her back and slid down off her mother's lap to the floor. Lillian looked around for something for her to play with.

"Look in the basement way. There should be a box with wooden pieces in it that she can build with."

They got Marcie situated between them on the kitchen floor. Lillian watched her as she happily pulled blocks out and stacked them up. She knew she had to tell Millie what had happened. But, saying out loud to her that she wanted to leave Morris made it more real. Was she really going to leave him? Impossible. Her head hurt.

"He hit me."

She looked Millie right in the eye, and a little fence appeared and stood neatly around her heart. There was something a little bit strong there. Millie said nothing – just sat, waited, returned Lillian's direct look.

"He took my car keys, he told me I couldn't be in the play."

Lillian sat up straighter. Morris's deeds sounded downright villainous to her through the filter of Millie's scrutiny.

"Has he hit you before?"

"Not exactly. But, a couple of days ago he tightened my scarf around my neck so tight I couldn't breathe or swallow."

Millie frowned.

"He scares me. I don't know what he'll do if he finds me, but I don't think I want to find out. I think he'll hurt me. He already has. He thinks he owns me."

Millie listened, impassive.

"I've been with Harold, Millie. You know... *been* with."

Millie just listened.

"... So I know without a doubt that I don't ever want to be with Morris again."

Her eyes got big.

"I can't believe I'm saying these things out loud."

Inside, the fence around her heart became a solid wall. It was a protection from somewhere. Lillian reached down to add a block to Marcie's stack.

With great effort, Millie hoisted herself out of her chair and drew a glass of water from the tap, then handed it to Lillian.

"So, he hit you. Where? What happened?"

As she talked to Millie about all that had gone on in the last few days, Lillian lit a cigarette, took a big drag, then set it in the ashtray and rubbed her hair dry with the towel. When she got to the part about being knocked down by Morris in their bedroom, she stood, opened her bathrobe and displayed the evidence.

Millie scooped portions of chicken pot pie into bowls, then stopped what she was doing to really look at Lillian's bruise. Her mouth took on a grim, determined aspect. She looked like she had plenty to say.

"Are you sure you want to do what you're talking about doing? Leave Morris? Leave your life here in Mason City and start another one somewhere else? It's not going to be easy, Lillian. What about Marcie? How will you support the two of you?"

Lillian closed her robe and sat down.

"You know what, Millie? I'm a college graduate. I'm sure I can support us."

She said it, but she didn't necessarily believe it.

Millie set a bowl on the table in front of Lillian and Marcie immediately scrambled onto her mother's lap. Lillian wrapped her arms around her daughter then crushed her cigarette out in the ashtray.

"Wait a minute, honey, it's too hot."

A strong gust of wind blew rain noisily against the window over the sink and both women turned to see it. Daylight faded. It was past four o'clock.

"Support yourself? Doing what? You can't be a teacher with a child. Who will watch her while you work if you're a clerk or a secretary? What else is there? I suppose you could work in a factory."

Lillian stirred the pot pie then blew on a small bite. Marcie took it happily.

"The only thing I'm really good at is being an actress, and what kind of life would that be for a child?"

"Well, I don't know..."

Millie eased herself down at the table and worked her food with a spoon.

"It might be a pretty interesting one, Lil."

A flutter of excitement ignited inside Lillian. An actress? A working actress? She set her spoon down and looked cautiously at Millie.

"Where?"

"There're theaters everywhere you know... Omaha, Chicago, Minneapolis, even Des Moines. Then, of course, there's New York City and places East."

Millie held her spoon delicately, with her pinkie up, and took a big bite. She closed her eyes while she chewed – took great pleasure in the eating of her own creation.

Lillian's mind began to move in a fast forward direction.

"I'll need an apartment, Millie… or, at least a room with a hot plate."

"YWCA? It's always a good place to get started, and all those cities have one, I'm sure."

"And, someone to watch Marcie, preferably close to the theater where I'll be working, maybe even someone helping with the play, and…"

She saw herself bow on a stage; in her arms – a bouquet of flowers. Then she imagined herself in her own little kitchen with Marcie at her feet, the radio from the front room… lace curtains, a plant on the table.

"Whoa, girl. Hold on. It's an idea with possibilities, but you have to be practical."

Lillian's eyes shone. It was a way out. There actually was something she could do in the world that could bring money in. She didn't need a man to support her. She could do it herself. In her heart, trumpets played a fanfare surrounded by golden light.

"This is it, Millie. I can do this! I just don't know how, yet. Oh, thank you for helping me. Thank you so much."

"It looks to me like you're sitting in a kitchen in the middle of Iowa, my dear. You're not quite there yet."

But, she smiled conspiratorially at Lillian who reached across the table and took a hold of her hand. The young woman trembled with excitement.

"If I'm going to leave town without Morris knowing about it, I'll need a disguise. I don't want him or anyone else to know anything about where I'm going. If he finds out, he might kill me – and I'm not kidding. And, even if he doesn't kill me in body, he'll kill my spirit. And my spirit rebels at that idea."

They both laughed.

"I won't let him. Period."

For a moment, the two women looked right into each others' eyes. They both knew that what Lillian said was true.

"If he comes around here asking, you won't tell will you?"

Millie slapped the table.

"Ha. It'll be a snowy day in hell before I tell your husband where you went, my dear. Don't you worry."

Marcie stirred food out of the bowl onto the table with the big spoon.

"Here baby, climb down now."

Lillian disengaged the child from her lap and stood her on the floor. Marcie immediately sat and began to play with the blocks again.

"You'll need a whole new personality, at least long enough to get away from Mason City."

"Well, have no fear."

Lillian's eyes were bright. She pointed one finger into the air, one hand across her heart.

"I... am an actress."

19

In lieu of a plan, Morris fled upstairs to the bathroom and barely made it in time to assuage the griping of his bowels. He blamed Lillian. She was causing so much disruption to his normal routine that his entire system was out of whack. That woman had some answering to do, by God. And, what about his special time with his daughter? He always had the option to spend an hour on Sunday afternoons with her to read a book or build with blocks. A clammy layer of perspiration erupted across his forehead as he struggled on the toilet. This whole thing was meshugah. As soon as Lillian came home, he would set her straight. He leaned forward, elbows on knees, and cradled his head in his hands.

Morris was deep in thought and bodily upheaval when the telephone rang. He sprang to attention but was slowed in his scramble to answer the incessant ring by his inebriated and indelicate state.

He flew down the stairs, swung around the banister with one hand, held his pants up with the other, and made it to the phone moments after the last ring had died out.

"Hello? Hello?"

He shouted into the phone but heard only the dial tone, then slammed it down into the cradle.

In the quiet hall next to the kitchen, Morris stood, head down, and wondered who had called and what to do next. He could put the radio on, although all they were talking about was how bad things were and how everyone was about to lose all their money. He picked up his head and looked out the back door window. Rain... cold rain and wind. His hands fumbled as he tucked in his shirt and fastened his pants.

On his way to the living room he stopped at the front door to pick the paper up off the floor, then opened the door. The yellow paint from last night's offense had run in streaks off the words down to the bottom. He touched a sticky spot and his finger came away yellow. There had been other desecrations and illegal activity by the local KKK recently. Those hoodlums would never be brought to justice, though. In Mason City, the most that would happen would be a report filed with the police and maybe a small mention buried in the local section of the paper. There was no way to prosecute if no one had seen it happen. He would talk to the boys at the store in the morning, have them refinish the door, or do whatever they needed to do to restore it... first thing in the morning. Not many people were out today. It would hardly be seen.

In the living room he laid down on the davenport and opened the paper. Ten seconds later he sat up and threw it down onto the floor. Who on earth could he talk to? What about Leonard Shapiro? His wife, Sylvia, knew everything about everyone in town. Morris couldn't stand her. But, maybe she would have a clue as to Lillian's whereabouts. The question was, how could he find out what he wanted to know from her without letting her know that Lillian was missing?

He paced back and forth in the living room, cleared his throat and smoothed his hair back at his temples several times. Should he phone them or just go over. They lived close by – a few houses down on Maple. He decided to make a friendly visit. He could talk about last night's appalling affront and somehow lead the conversation around to Lillian. She could be out with a friend. That wasn't so unusual. Or, she could be visiting his mother with the baby. Yes, that was it.

Despite an unsettled gut, Morris stopped at the liquor cabinet on his way out and poured himself a shot of whiskey. Best to be braced before venturing forth in lousy weather.

Even with his hat and raincoat on, Morris couldn't escape rain down his neck as he walked rapidly up the sidewalk to the Shapiro's. Their house was new, too – only a couple of years old. But, it wasn't as big as Morris', nor was their back yard as nice.

At their door he rapped three times with his knuckles, then waited. The damn weather. He was frozen.

The door opened and a surprised Leonard quickly ushered Morris in with a handshake.

"Come in, man. Good to see you. What are you doing out today?"

Morris shook his hat off.

"Hello, Leonard. Thought I'd pay a visit. Things are quiet at home. Lillian's visiting my mother with the baby."

He undid his coat and handed it to Leonard.

"What are you up to?"

Morris didn't notice, but Leonard was suspicious. In the two years since they had moved into practically adjacent houses, Morris had never stopped by unexpectedly. He didn't look good, either. Leonard thought he looked pale and nervous. He hung the coat in the closet and set the hat on a rack, then ushered them into the living room and walked over to turn the radio off. The Sunday paper lay in disarray on the floor next to the easy chair, and a green striped afghan showed signs of recent use on the davenport.

"Quite a bad deal at your house last night, eh?"

Was that just last night?

"Those damn thugs. They shouldn't get away with it."

Morris looked at the yellow paint that had dried on his finger, then up at Leonard, who watched him closely.

"They wear those hoods so nobody can recognize them."

Leonard stood with hands in pockets.

"Hmm. Hard to prosecute."

"Levinson said they never did catch the ones who did it to him. Not even a lead. Do the police give a damn?"

"Well, you'd think they would."

Leonard folded his arms.

"Jews make up a large percentage of the merchants in this town. Even if it wasn't wrong from a human standpoint, one would hope that the police, or at least Mayor Grundwald, would find it advantageous from an economic standpoint to make life here for us less, shall we say, difficult."

"Does this kind of thing have to follow us everywhere we go?"

Out the window, Morris watched a car bump down the street in the rain filled potholes. They'd been trying to get Forest Glade paved for more than a year.

"Well, we know this isn't going to run any Jews out of town. If that's all they do, burn stars in the yard and throw some paint on the door, we'll be okay. I suppose with the economy going to hell, they'll want to blame someone. Why not Jews? Why should this day be different from any other day? What're you going to do about your lawn?"

Morris was impatient, his belly churned.

"I'll call the boys out from the store in the morning."

He dismissed it with a wave of his hand.

"They'll throw some sod down. I'll have to have the front door refinished."

"Good. That's good. Have a seat, Morris. Make yourself comfortable. Let me get you something to drink... a soda pop?"

"Do you have any scotch? I could use one right now."

Morris walked rigidly, like a robot, to the chair, then sat. In his bowels, a somersault turned. He needed a drink.

Leonard had never seen him like this.

"It's only three o'clock in the afternoon. Are you sure? I can offer you some coffee or a..."

"No thanks, just a shot of whiskey if you've got it."

"Sure."

When Leonard left the room, Morris stood and walked over to the mantle to look at an array of framed photographs. Sylvia Shapiro wasn't bad looking, but she was too thin and wore too much makeup. And, when she smiled, her mouth looked huge under her hook nose... like a clown bird. Actually, she did look like a bird – a stork, with those thin legs.

"Here you go, sir."

Morris spun around and took the drink.

"Thank you. Is Sylvia around?"

Leonard looked more closely at Morris.

"Are you alright, Scharf? Do you feel okay?"

Morris shot his eyes around the room. He wasn't interested in this small talk.

"Yes, yes, I'm fine. Not happy with the general state of affairs in the world, but, then, I don't suppose anyone is."

He looked into the hallway from where he stood.

"Is your wife home?"

For a moment, Leonard just looked at Morris. Then, he nodded and left the room again. Morris sat and heard him walk up the stairs and call for his wife. They talked upstairs but he couldn't make out what they said. When they came into the living room, he tipped his head back and finished his drink, then stood.

"Hello, Sylvia. How are you?"

Sylvia, who was from the East, reached out to shake hands with Morris.

"I'm fine, Morris. But, you look like you're not having a good day. What's going on?"

He shook her hand, but Morris didn't like her forwardness. Plus, she had that New York twang in her voice. He feigned a smile.

"I've felt better, thank you. Nothing's going on. I thought I'd come by."

Sylvia gestured for them to sit, which he did – with his hands under his thighs to keep them steady.

For what seemed like an hour, but was actually only a few seconds, no one said anything. Sylvia and Leonard waited, watched. Morris sought an avenue.

"Um, lousy weather."

Sylvia blinked once then folded her hands together.

"Do you need something, Morris? How can we help you?"

This was the part that Morris had failed to prepare for. How exactly should he ask about Lillian? Was Sylvia in the Ladies' Club? Did Lillian need anything at their store, the Hitching Post? What about the play? Did she know anything about that? There was something fishy going on there. He belched into his fist which prompted a large, sicky gas bubble to gurgle its way down through him and nearly out. His eyes shot open, he sat up straight.

Sylvia and Leonard exchanged a look. Morris took a shot in the dark.

"Have you and Lillian seen much of each other lately?"

At Sylvia's surprised face, Morris blurted out.

"I'm trying to decide what to get her for her birthday next month. I thought you might have an idea, considering you probably know what she's been up to."

A clammy film of sweat erupted over his entire body. Both Sylvia and Leonard looked warily at Morris as he searched for ideas.

"What about the play she's in? Do you know anything about that?"

"Who are you, the District Attorney?"

Sylvia pursed her lips. If she wasn't mistaken, Morris was tipsy. She curled both legs up under her in the chair and nonchalantly lit a cigarette which infuriated Morris. Why was she taking so long to answer? But, he was after information… best to play along.

"Yes, I guess you could say that."

His mind scurried around while he gingerly adjusted himself in the chair.

"I was hoping to talk to the director, see what Scharf and Sons can offer in the way of assistance."

Not bad for the spur of the moment.

Leonard got up to check something at the back of the heater which stood in a corner. Sylvia puffed out a big O of smoke, crossed her bird legs and swung one right at Morris.

"I thought you were trying to figure out a birthday present for her."

"Oh, yes… yes, that's true, too."

Heavy rain created a constant humming undertone in the

room. Morris didn't like how the Shapiros both left large spaces in the conversation. He kept up his part, why didn't they? Plus, he had to exert constant vigilance in order to maintain control down below.

Sylvia tipped her head and looked thoughtfully at Morris, then finally spoke.

"Do you know the director, Harold Winston?"

Aha! Harold Winston.

"No, I don't know him personally..."

His voice cracked.

"But I believe Lillian has spoken highly of him."

He wanted to spit a bad taste out of his mouth.

"He would be the one to talk to... he or Moody Luckle. Moody takes care of lots of the details for the plays. He came by the store looking for some empty boxes the other day."

From behind the heater, Leonard spoke up.

"My wife's a fount of useful information, Morris."

"That's alright."

Morris felt magnanimous. He had what he needed. Let her blather on.

"I don't know much else about the play except that it's slated to open in early December. I do know that Harold Winston's wife is down in Independence. She's crazy, they say. He's done work at the high school in the theater department, too."

Morris stood and mentally checked the security of his bodily functions. If he left immediately, he could make it home.

"Thank you both for a fine visit. I must be leaving

now."

To keep up an appearance of self-control, he strode abruptly to the front door, and before either Sylvia or Leonard could recover their surprise to do it for him, he retrieved his coat and hat and exited their house. He ran the four doors down the sidewalk to his own and barely made it up the stairs and into the bathroom before all hell broke loose again.

When he was finished, Morris stumbled weakly into his bedroom and fell across the bed. Before he passed out, he noticed that it hadn't been made up, and the vague thought floated through that his wife was definitely not holding up her end of the bargain.

20

Millie squinted her eyes at Lillian for a moment, then sat back and slapped her thigh with her hand.

"Well, I'll be. You are something, Mrs. Scharf. Or, should I say, Miss Rosenheim? Who do you want to be next?"

The two women laughed and suddenly there was a new energy in Millie's kitchen. Anything seemed possible to Lillian. As she ate a few bites of the delicious food, the ideas flew toward them like rays of warm sunshine cutting through the rain and fog.

"I've always wanted to visit Chicago."

"There's a train heading east at 5:30. That doesn't give

us much time. You need to be someone unrecognizable, Lil. You're traveling with a small child, too. Do you have any money?"

Lillian told her about Harold's generous gift. They decided that two hundred and fifty dollars, plus the thirty eight she already had would be more than enough to get her there, rent a room with, and buy a few essentials for the two of them. She would seek actor's try-outs immediately and lug Marcie along with her if she had to.

Marcie stood up, fussed and tugged on her own little pants.

"Oh, for heaven's sake, I haven't changed her in hours."

Lillian looked abruptly at Millie.

"What about diapers? I only have three more clean ones."

Millie didn't hesitate.

"Don't worry about that, Lil. I have plenty of supplies... look around."

She motioned to the stacks of fabric piled everywhere, among other collected treasures.

"I even have an oilcloth satchel that you can use to carry the dirty ones in 'til you can get there and wash them out."

Lillian picked up her baby and waltzed around the kitchen table with her. She hadn't felt this hopeful in a long time. While she changed Marcie, her mother's face floated into her awareness, and with it, a vision of an old woman – stooped over – who led a little child by the hand. When she shared her idea with Millie, the hefty woman nodded thoughtfully.

"We can make you look like an old woman, Lil, but it'll

be up to you to convince the Mason City people and the people on the train, at least, that you really are one."

With the second safety pin securely fastened, Lillian pulled up the rubber pants.

"Don't worry about that for a second. I actually played an old woman in college... I've had practice. And, now I have a limp. It'll be perfect."

She smiled, a novelty of late for her face.

"What about Marcie, though? If someone between here and the train station recognizes either of us, we'll be found out. I want a clean get-away, Millie... no clues left behind."

"Don't worry, my dear. I have an idea."

The two women worked well as a team. There was an old wicker baby buggy on the back porch that they brought in and cleaned up. Millie dug around in her closets for the right dress as Lillian struggled with padding that would make her look older. Fortunately, Millie had done costumes for plays for more than twenty years, as the clutter in her home could testify. She worked with needle and thread – assured a good fit for the large dress on Lillian's normally slender, now well-padded body. A curly gray wig was brought out from the back of a closet, and the oilcloth satchel, along with an outdated handbag and a cane, began to complete the ensemble.

Marcie was trickier. They both watched her play on the floor and tried to imagine a disguise for a toddler.

"That's a recognizable face right there."

Millie tapped two fingernails against the counter.

"How about we turn her into a boy?"

Lillian's first reaction was distaste. Her beautiful little girl... a boy? Millie went on.

"If we cut her hair real short and dirty up her cheeks a little, I think it would work. We'll have to dress her like a boy, too. I think there's a pair of child's overalls here, somewhere."

As she pulled boxes off of shelves in the bedroom, Lillian sat in front of the dresser mirror and applied a heavy layer of pancake makeup to her face.

"Here, try this."

Millie held up a dusty old black hat with a wide brim from the era of Lillian's mother. It had a crushed purple silk flower stuck into the band in the front. She stood behind Lillian and placed it down over the wig, then tugged it at an angle.

They both gazed in the mirror at the frumpy, elderly woman who sat before them.

"It's good, Millie. I'm almost done with my make up. Then we need to get Marcie ready."

Lillian turned in her chair and took a hold of Millie's hand again. She had tears in her eyes, but they were happiness tears this time.

"How can I ever thank you for what you're doing for me, Millie?"

A sparkle gathered in the corner of Millie's eyes, too.

"Just succeed, honey... that's all. Helping you escape is one of the finer things I've ever done. Then, some day, when you're in a position to help another woman, I know you'll do that. It's how we women get along in the world."

"Yeah, who needs men, anyway?"

Millie knocked gently on the top of Lillian's head.

"Yes, that's absolutely true for some women, Lil. But, remember, the world is run by men. It's in your best interest to understand them and get along with them the best you can. My friend, Carrie Chapman Catt, taught me that. She worked hard in this man's world to get the vote for women. As she said, all men aren't awful... just most of them."

A corner of Lillian's mouth turned up, but that was all. She didn't want to think about the great big world out there that she was about to launch herself into. Getting out of town undetected was trial enough. She pushed thoughts of Morris, Harold and her life in Mason City far back behind the more pressing issues at hand.

As Millie pedaled her sewing machine, Lillian pursued the ticklish part of their plan. They decided to get Marcie drunk so that she would sleep through the get-away. Lillian tried whiskey, which Marcie spat out immediately, then beer, which she seemed to like.

"Millie, I know that even though it's prohibition, everyone has plenty of liquor in their house. But, how did you get this beer?"

Millie snickered.

"Ha. I love beer, and my friend, Amos Hofstad, knows it. He makes all kinds, too, raspberry and dandelion. The stuff she's drinking is huckleberry beer. Taste it, it's good."

Lillian took a sip from the glass, but Marcie grabbed her arms and pulled them down. She wanted to drink it.

"Okay, honey. Good girl. Drink up."

Ten minutes later, a tipsy Marcie stood transfixed – stared out the front window at the rain, as her mother kept her head still for Millie's shears. It gave Lillian a small pang to watch her daughter's beautiful curls fall to the floor, but it also gave her a thrill. In less than forty minutes she would be on the Rocket to Chicago to start her new life. She was going to leave everyone and everything behind. It was a monumentally huge step – biggest of her life.

They would arrive early Monday morning in a brand new city, so she and Millie discussed every detail they could think of in preparation.

"What's your story going to be Lil?"

Millie snipped close to the baby's scalp.

"What do you mean?"

"Are you this little boy's grandmother, come to fetch him from protective custody after his parents were killed in a car crash in St. Ansgar to take him home with you to Chicago?"

Lillian turned Marcie around to face the scissors better.

"Uh, sure… yeah, Millie. That's good. I'll use that. His name needs to be Marcel or Mark or something like Marcie so she'll answer. I think Mark."

"Okay, and what's your name going to be?"

"Well, let's name me for your friend Carrie Chapman Catt. How about… Mary Chapman?"

"It's a nice plain name."

Millie snipped carefully near the child's face.

"I think you need to stay in character until you get to Chicago. That way you won't be able to be traced. But, you'll want to rent the room as Lillian."

"I'll change my clothes at the train station when I get there, but I think I should change my real name, too. I could be Mary Chapman. Could it be that easy?"

"I don't see why not. Sounds good, Mary Chapman. Let's put your clothes in the foot of the buggy along with some spare diapers. I'll pack you some things to eat... you can carry those in the diaper bag."

They turned Marcie once more around to finish her other side. Lillian continued to feed her beer. She searched for all possible unanswered questions.

"Can I take the buggy on the train?"

"Oh, sure, the porter will store it for you."

Every detail was covered. They found an old pair of button-up boots, like something her mother might have worn as a young woman. They were perfect for the costume, as was the string of fake pearls Millie hung around her neck.

When her hair was all cut off, Marcie danced wildly and happily around the room, her hands in the air. Both Lillian and Millie joined in her gleeful exuberance. Bent over the cane, and although she looked much more like someone's dowdy old grandma than herself, Lillian tapped a tasty rhythm onto the wood floor. Millie swung little Marcie around once too many times. The child's projectile vomit exploded down the front of her. Both women laughed until they were nearly hysterical. As soon as she had thrown up, Marcie snuggled into a corner of the davenport and went to sleep.

It was 5:00... time to make their way to the train station. The rain hadn't let up, but Lillian's spirits couldn't be dampened. What a different day this was turning out to be from how it had started. She would never have to see Morris again because Chicago was big enough to disappear in, for sure.

After Millie cleaned up and their final preparatory details were covered, the two women wrestled the buggy into the backseat of Millie's old Ford. Lillian hoisted the newly minted Mark into the buggy and decided not to give any more thought to the pain in her hip. The new Mary Chapman gathered herself into Millie's car. Millie shut her door then lumbered around to the driver's seat in the rain, her thin, wet hair plastered against her skull. She turned to Lillian.

"You're almost home free, honey. Twenty-five minutes to go and you're a free woman."

Lillian dug a cigarette out of her purse and lit it up. Inside of her, a tangle of fear and excitement. There was no way Morris would ever know that she had taken the train out of town. Despite her repeated attempts to calm herself with that truth, she knew she wouldn't breathe easy until the train rolled out of Mason City with Mary Chapman and her grandson, Mark, safely ensconced inside.

21

An hour passed. Morris dreamed he was Noah, giving orders on the ark. Everyone looked up to him, God was happy with him. Then, instantly, he was a small, helpless, pig-like animal being swept from one end of the deck to another by the stormy sea. He washed overboard, squealed loudly, flailed in the deep water for a breath of air.

He awoke tangled in the bed sheets and scrambled to free himself with a gigantic fear lodged in his body. For several minutes he lay still – tried to hear the sounds of Lillian downstairs over the pounding of his own heart. The rain had not subsided but it was darker out, darker than normal for, what was it? He checked the clock: 4:15 in the afternoon. Except for the constant rain that drummed on the roof, the house was completely quiet.

A cramp grabbed him in the middle and he curled up. Then he stuffed a corner of the bed sheet into his mouth and let out a muffled and truly fearful howl. Where was Lillian? Where was his God? He closed his eyes and sent up a prayer, in Hebrew, to the holy one.

Blessed art Thou, oh Lord our God, King of the Universe, who has sanctified us by Thy Commandments... bring home my wife. I am your faithful servant, oh Lord. I ask you to answer my prayer and bring my wayward wife safely home where she belongs. Amen.

A calmness entered Morris. The fear from moments ago subsided. He returned to the bathroom, took two aspirin, washed his face, brushed his teeth and hair. Before he went down, he assessed his looks in the mirror. Such a fine looking man he was... a leader in the community. He stood up straighter. Morris Scharf was a man to be reckoned with. Now, who was this Winston fellow?

Downstairs, he picked up the telephone.

"Hello? Lavonne? Do you have a number for a Harold Winston?

"Just a moment, please, Mr. Scharf."

He looked into the quiet, darkened kitchen where a wooden toy horse lay forgotten under the high chair.

"I have the number, sir. Would you like me to connect you?"

"Uh, no, thank you, Lavonne. Why don't you just give it to me? And, how about the address, too, if you don't mind?"

"Alright, sir. The number is Garden 3-4937. And, the address is 304 Rockland. Will that be all?"

Morris wrote as she spoke.

"Yes, thank you, Lavonne. That will be all."

He hung up. Rockland was on the other side of town. Should he call the man? What should he say? That his wife was missing and did he know where she might be? He had a bad feeling about Winston. Lillian had been happy, radiant really, when she came home from her rehearsals. He knew she loved to act, but something else gnawed at the edges of him.

Morris massaged his ragged belly as he paced through the kitchen. This play was the only thing that was different in Lillian's life. And, since it had started, she had changed. Why, his father in law told him yesterday that she wanted to leave him! Morris stopped. Humiliation fell like a veil down through him. She wanted to leave him. This man, this Harold Winston, had something to do with it. Not just something, but, a lot. And, his own father-in-law had delivered the news!

As darkness seeped into the Scharf home at 32 Woodshire Drive, Morris gathered his coat and hat and prepared to go out, yet again, in search of his wife. He downed another shot of whiskey, staggered sideways toward the wall and landed against his shoulder with his hands over his face. The idea that his own wife might be having an impropriety with another man was so abhorrent to him that he couldn't let himself get all the way to that thought.

Instead, he braced up. If she and this Harold Winston

were being drawn to each other, then he was completely correct to end her participation in the play. As for Winston, he would just set the man straight in no uncertain terms. He breathed deeply, then put his hat on. The room swirled around him.

Luckily, Morris had grown up in Mason City. Even in his inebriated state, he found that if he drove slowly and aimed the car in the general direction of the east side, he could, by childhood instinct, navigate correctly through each intersection as it came up.

On Rockland, when he angled the car toward the curb to read the house numbers, the right front tire hit and Morris instantly recoiled his feet up off the pedals. The car lurched forward then snapped back in a stop and his head flew in unison. The upheaval unnerved him and he blurted out a quick sob. Lillian... Lillian in the kitchen at the sink, sitting on her stool, talking on the telephone. Lillian dressed up for dinner out at Costa's... those red lips... those hips under the covers... those full breasts...

He yanked the door handle down and unfolded waveringly out of the car. For nearly half a minute he stood where he was and ostensibly gazed at the house of Harold Winston, whoever he was.

But it was the image of Lillian's smooth, round bottom that hovered in his forebrain... that woman, those parts, belonged to him. What good fortune for him to have such a woman. He spread her legs and pushed himself right into her as a strong gust of wind sent a drenching splatter against him. He shook his coat and took a crooked path to the front door, along with the vision of his wife that lingered.

When Harold opened his front door, both men stood and stared before either one spoke. Harold saw who he had a feeling was a crazed Morris Scharf. Who else would knock on his door on this particular day with black curly hair and look so Jewish?

Morris saw a Ferris wheel of blonde men roll around in front of him. He blinked hard to stabilize, but it wouldn't, couldn't happen, then he leaned forward and threw up – splattered on the edge of the welcome mat and the toes of Harold's house shoes. His body leaned sideways and he slid along the doorjamb until he squatted under the portico which gave little protection from the windy rain.

Harold left, returned with new slippers and a towel and cleaned up the mess. Then, he pulled and coaxed and managed to maneuver Morris into his living room where the man's wife had been a few hours earlier. Puddles formed on the floor under Morris as he sat with arms braced against the sides of the chair and tried to mollify the effects of the heaving room.

Harold gave him a glass of water and a small towel, then sat across from him on the davenport.

"Morris Scharf, right?"

Morris looked up at Harold and saw his face circle in front of him. He could only afford a quick nod. He spoke through thick lips.

"Winston."

"Yes, I'm Harold Winston."

Harold was not impressed with pale, clammy, clearly inebriated Morris Scharf. He sat silent and waited for

Morris to say something else. Finally, Morris picked his head up again and spoke, but only in short, tight-lipped bursts.

"Lillian... my wife... looking... for her."

Morris tried to look Winston in the eye, but there were too many eyes to follow. His head lolled back against the back of the chair, which stopped the motion of his head. But, in his mind he continued on backward in a large, cosmic roll.

"Say, Scharf. Wake up."

Harold shook him by the shoulder.

"...saw your wife, Lillian."

When Morris opened his eyes, the room spun, but he sat up straighter. Harold handed him a cup of coffee, brought his hands up from his lap one at a time and wrapped them around the mug.

"Here you go… try this."

The man needed help.

While Morris blew on his coffee, Harold watched him and thought about his own dilemma. A man surely had a right to know where his wife was, if she wanted him to know. But, he knew that that was not what Lillian wanted.

He felt pity for the man. Who knew what really went on between two people? And to have a woman leave you, one as lovely as Lillian, well, even if you caused it, it was still a horrendous thing.

Harold went into the kitchen, lit a cigarette and leaned against the counter under the window. This kind of stormy, cold day always brought up a pang of loneliness. He had known he couldn't keep Lillian Scharf. She had her own life; a husband, a child. But, for a few days, a deeply buried happiness in Harold had been rekindled by a beautiful and generous woman. He was grateful to her. And, if this Scharf hadn't been such a lout, it never could have happened. He stubbed his cigarette out in the ashtray. He didn't know how much Morris knew. He would play dumb.

Morris dreamed he ran a gauntlet on a ship. He leapt off the plank and hovered over the water, electrocuted by fear. Then, a man's voice cut through.

"Wake up, Scharf."

Harold shook his shoulder again.

"Wake up, you're dreaming."

Morris was glad to open his eyes; glad he was slouched on a davenport and not about to drown.

"Bathroom?"

Harold pointed and Morris stumbled his way there. He used the toilet, ran cold water, cupped his hands and rinsed his mouth out and then his face. In the mirror, his worried face, sweaty and pale, peered out. He stood up straight and, with feet braced against vertigo, tucked his shirt in, pulled each sleeve of his sweater down over his wrists and smoothed the hair back at his temples. Despite the swirling around him, he was determined to appear controlled.

He stood behind a living room chair with one hand on the back for support, cleared his throat and assumed an imperious stance.

"Did I hear you say you have seen my wife?"

To Harold, he appeared the buffoon. Was this guy really going to bully him into telling him about Lillian?

"I saw her earlier today."

Morris's eyes shot open then he squinted menacingly. Harold was not afraid.

"Where, uh, why?"

He tipped his chin down to threaten.

"Do you know where she is now?"

An easy one for Harold.

"No."

This was not what Morris expected.

"Where did you see her, my wife?"

He emphasized the last word.

"She was here."

"Here? In your house?"

Morris struggled to maintain composure. What had Lillian been doing in this man's house?

"She rang the doorbell and it was raining so I let her in. She had Marcie with her."

The familiarity in the man's voice was too much for Morris. He folded his arms then quickly unfolded them. Both palms smoothed hair back at his temples, but a sheen of moisture remained on his forehead.

"What in God's name was she doing here?"

He stomped his foot and a half snort, half sob burped out of him.

Harold was struck with pity again for such a man. He obviously didn't know about the two of them... thank God for small favors... but there was going to be no good way out of this mess for the fellow. He tried to soften what he had to say.

"Listen, Scharf. She came here because I direct her in

the play. We're friends..."

"Friends? She's *friends* with you? Since when is my wife *friends* with another man?"

A ruddy color rose up his neck and he could barely find enough air to propel his words out.

"Wh-where is she now? Where is she?"

Harold hunched his shoulders with his palms up.

"I couldn't really say."

Morris sputtered.

"Well, where did she go when she left here?"

He turned abruptly and stepped to the front window – watched a large drip make its way down the glass. A moment later, the streetlight blinked once then came on. Both men stood in the evening light and listened as the small clock chimed five times from the bedroom. Scharf's distress moved Harold. He could help him.

"How about if I drive you to where I took her? You don't look like you're in much shape to drive."

"Where did you take her?"

"To Millie Blovak's house. But it was hours ago."

Morris reeled around and glared at Harold.

"Why would she go to Millie Blovak's house – on a Sunday?"

Harold walked into his bedroom for his shoes and jacket and answered Morris from in there.

"That's where she wanted to go. So, that's where I took her."

Morris bit furiously at a hangnail, spit it out and watched it land on the curtain. His insides churned and he ran around and sat on the chair. He was close. He could tell. It was just a matter of time and he would have this whole thing figured out.

When Harold came back in the room, Morris stood, straightened his sweater, and with the help of Harold Winston, donned his coat and hat, and the two men headed out. It was 5:05.

22

Lillian wasted no time. The moment she was seated in Millie's car she began the process of becoming the old woman she was turning into.

"Ask me some questions, Millie, so I can practice my new voice."

"Okay. Sure. Let's see. Where are you off to on this rainy evening, ma'am?"

Lillian lowered her voice, slowed it down and added a thickness, a maturity, to it.

"Oh, I'm goin' back home, thanks."

She took a drag off her cigarette, cracked the window and blew smoke out, then looked over at Millie.

"How was that?"

"Sounds good. Remember that you're probably older than everyone which gives you an advantage in conversation. If you don't like the question, be evasive."

They smiled at each other.

A guarded euphoria waited impatiently behind Lillian's nervousness. Twenty minutes more and she was home free. Could it really be this easy to leave Morris? To leave everything and everyone she knew behind her? All of her thoughts and efforts of the moment were focused on becoming her character, old Mary Chapman from Chicago.

As she scratched a spot under the edge of her wig, she envisioned a singular version of the older women she passed daily downtown; slightly bent over, with a cane and an almost imperceptible limp. Her Mary would be practical, a church lady, with a no-nonsense approach. Yes, her daughter had been killed, her son-in-law, too, in a car-train crash, but the child needed to be raised and she was certainly the one to do it.

"This is a big part for me, Millie... Mary Chapman."

"Biggest of your life?"

Lillian grimaced.

"I never thought my life would change this much this fast. Ever since Harold and the play, everything's different... everything. And, it all happened so fast."

Millie leaned forward to see better out of the windshield. The wipers barely kept up.

"Do you think Morris has changed, too?"

Lillian smoked and fingered the silk flower on the hat in her lap.

"I think he's becoming more of who he is, the same as I am."

Millie looked over at Lillian, who really did look seventy years old.

"But...."

"But, I don't like who he's turning into. I guess maybe I didn't ever like him that much to begin with."

Millie shrugged her shoulders.

"You'll have plenty of time after you get settled in Chicago to figure it all out. And, from what I can tell, a person never really does understand the whole thing. Everyone's complex and each marriage has it's own inside story, which, of course, is different depending on who you're talking to."

She shifted into third then reached over and took Lillian's hand, gave it a squeeze.

"You're going to do just fine, Lillian. If anyone can pull this off, it's you. I'm rooting for you all the way."

Lillian squeezed back and swallowed down a lump in her throat. She couldn't say anything. Up ahead, the lights from the train station welcomed them as they pulled up to park under the portico.

Just as Millie's car rounded the corner and headed toward the train station, Harold turned his car onto her street at the other end of the block. The wipers kept time as he pulled up in front of her house and put his car in neutral. Morris sat dumbfounded as both men peered through the rain at the darkened house. Finally, Harold spoke.

"It looks like no one's home. Everything's dark."

Morris' head spun.

"This is where you brought her? When?"

"Well, let's see..."

How much should he divulge? It couldn't hurt for Scharf to know what time Lillian was here. Besides, where was she, anyway? He wanted to know, too.

"It was around three, maybe a little after."

Morris clung to the arm rest on the door.

"What time is it now?"

"Well, it must be about 5:15."

Morris peered through the rain at the house and swallowed his nausea down. To Harold, Scharf looked so forlorn and pathetic that his heart went out to him. He tried to help. He said the only thing he could think of.

"Maybe she's at the train station...."

Morris spun his head around so fast that he had to lay it back against the seat. He spoke in a harsh, angry whisper.

"Why do you say that? Why would she be there?"

Harold realized his mistake too late.

"Uh, just a lousy idea, Scharf. No real reason...."

"The 5:30 to Chicago? Let's go... now!"

He turned his head and glared at Winston. Nothing made sense to him, but the man obviously knew more than he let on.

Harold cleared his voice and put the car in gear.

"It was just a hunch. She's probably at your house by now."

He hoped, for her sake, that she wasn't, but he also hoped she wasn't at the train station, either. How terrible would it be for him to pull up there with her husband to find her waiting for the train?

"Well, the station's on the way to my house. Hurry up... we'll barely have enough time to get there."

Morris sat up rigid and straight, emboldened by this latest possibility.

The two women carefully removed the buggy from the back seat while Marcie slept, then faced each other to say goodbye. Lillian, with an oilcloth bag on one arm and a cane hung over her other wrist, found she couldn't talk or see very well... tears.

"It's okay, Lil. You're going to be fine. You just do what you need to do, now. Let me hear from you as soon as you're safe in Chicago. And, don't worry... I'm not giving your secret away... not ever."

Millie's eyes filled up, too.

As she reached around Millie to hug her, Lillian's voice came out in a whisper.

"Thank you, Millie. Thank you. You've done so much..."

Millie turned Lillian and herded her, along with the buggy, toward the door to the station.

"You're the one who's doing this. You're Mary Chapman now. You can do it. Good luck... you'll be fine."

Then, in a louder voice that reverberated through the station as she held the door...

"Goodbye, Mary. Take good care of little Mark. Have a safe trip. We'll be in touch."

23

Through the windows on the other side of the station, Lillian saw the train as it steamed and waited on the tracks. Just a few more minutes. She bent over the handle of the buggy and pushed it slowly toward the ticket window. She was on a stage in front of a full house – the curtain pulled back moments ago.

A short man with white hair parted down the middle and a neatly trimmed white mustache stood behind the iron bars at the counter. To Lillian he was a character in her play, the one she invented as she went along. In front of her, a middle aged woman bought a ticket, then leaned down, picked up a covered bird cage and went to sit near the door to the train. A tall man in a bowler stood and looked out the window with his hands folded behind his back.

Lillian limped to the ticket window, looked up out of her seventy year old face and talked to the ticket master with her seventy year old voice.

"Hello there. I'd like a ticket to Chicago, please."

She motioned with her cane to the buggy.

"My grandson's asleep. He's going with me."

No nonsense. Practical.

The man behind the counter didn't flinch.

"Yes Ma'am. That'll be seventeen dollars."

Lillian found her money and paid the man. As he handed her the ticket, her heart pulsed loudly in her ears. Just a few more steps and she would be safely out of the station and on the train. She could really use a cigarette.

Lillian wheeled the buggy to a bench near the door and checked on Marcie... out like a light. Good. They should be boarding any moment now.

Harold's car slid in the gravel as he swerved into a parking spot at the station. Morris flung the door open and lurched out into the rain like a flying scarecrow – ran through the rain and puddles to the portico and stopped underneath. He gathered himself together and smoothed his hair back. If Lillian was in there he would... what? He didn't want to make a scene. He would take her home. He would be reasonable and calm and she would take his arm and walk with him out of the station. A high pitched buzz grew in his head – his heart thudded fast and hard. Winston ran up and stood beside him.

It looked to Harold like Morris was about to cry – the man's face was all screwed up. Harold watched rain blow sideways across the parking lot. He didn't know what he'd do if he saw Lillian in the station. It was none of his business, really. He'd already said goodbye to her, and, unfortunately, Scharf was her husband. He counted on her not being in there – then he could take the fellow back to his house to get his car. Scharf wasn't quite as inebriated as before, even though he looked like hell. If he were playing the role of a drunken cuckold, he couldn't look any more the part, even down to his pale, clammy face. In the shadows, he looked crazed. Harold reached out and opened the station door.

Lillian kept track of every movement in the large room. All was quiet under the covered bird cage of the woman who waited on the bench across from her. On her bench, the man in the hat sat close enough that she smelled his mixture of toilet water and what she feared was just plain toilet. Marcie slept.

When the station master called out for the 5:30 to Chicago, Lillian turned to gather her things and saw Morris and Harold step inside the door to the station. Panic leapt up into her breast and bombarded around. She couldn't breathe. What were they doing together?

Morris looked absolutely deranged. So this had been an awful day for him, too. Lillian afforded herself a split second of satisfaction, but she didn't change her expression. Her job now was to get herself and her child out of the station and onto the train without Morris recognizing her.

As she slipped the straps of her bag over her wrist and took the cane in hand, she concentrated to make herself appear as the seventy year old Mary Chapman, not young Lillian Scharf (but she secretly kept her eye on them).

Morris wavered at the door, squinted and scanned the room with his eyes which travelled right over her and continued on around. When Harold's met hers, they stopped. He dropped his gaze down and up her body, the corner of his mouth pulled up wryly, then he looked right into her eyes. Her disguise was formidable. But Harold, who had spent his life in the theater, knew how to see through a facade... and this was Lillian. He lifted an eyebrow and gave her a surreptitious wink.

Morris swallowed but his throat was dry and stuck together. Lillian wasn't there. There was one man, a middle aged woman with a birdcage and a dumpy old woman with a stroller. Damn. He coughed then grabbed at his neck. He needed water and he needed a bathroom. He spotted a pitcher with several clean glasses on a table near the office and weaved his way toward them.

Lillian was mortified. She was exposed, completely naked, a sitting duck. Morris hadn't recognized her, but Harold certainly had. She gave a curt shake of her head 'no' to Harold and the strongest beseech to him with her eyes that she could come up with in one second. Morris clutched his neck and headed her way because, of course, she sat directly between him and the water. Lillian took a deep breath, let it out, then withdrew into the impermeable sheath of Mary Chapman.

Just as she took hold of the buggy handle, Morris loomed up in front of her. He looked terrible, frightening really... angry, red rimmed eyes, like a mad man.

"Pardon me...."

He waved his arms at the two women who sat across from each other.

"I need to get through here."

Lillian tried to maneuver the buggy out of his way but it wouldn't move. She jabbed it forward to free it just as Morris took a step. He tripped on the buggy's wheel, gave a loud whoop, then slipped and fell onto the floor. He lay for a moment on his back with his neck strained upwards then rolled onto his side and tried to get up, but slipped repeatedly in the wetness from his coat and shoes.

The smelly man stepped quickly over to him.

"Here you go. Let me help you."

He took a hold of Morris' arm and tried to lift him. But the floor was slippery and just as Morris gained a slight foothold, the man slipped, himself, and went down on a knee. Morris flung a hand out involuntarily to try to reach the bench but cracked his fingers hard against it instead. He let out a shriek and cradled his hurt hand with the other, then curled into a fetal position on the wet, dirty floor of the train station.

Lillian's instinct was to go to him. She looked up at Harold who had come over to help. He started to say something to her but she quickly shook her head no. At her feet, her husband writhed in pain – oblivious to her or anyone else. She watched as Harold put his hand on Morris. The other man climbed up onto the bench and wiped his hands on his coat.

"All aboard, all aboard for the 5:30 to Chicago."

Lillian turned around to check on her baby. Marcie roused – began to lift her head. Lillian reached down and stroked the child's head. She summoned a strong sleeping desire for her baby and sent the message out her palm – urged sleep back into her. In a second, Marcie relaxed down.

"Oh, my, my, my...."

Lillian renewed her dedication to her character as she fussed with her daughter's covers.

"Oh dear, oh my...."

She smoothed her dress, straightened her hat, checked the buggy for damage, tucked Marcie in again and, although she mostly wanted to ignore him, peeked over to catch a glimpse of Morris as he squirmed on the floor.

Nothing deep within stirred her to compassion. Their little family was over. Lillian looked at her daughter as she slept, and then at Morris. *No* father was better than *that* father. Why would she want that man to influence her daughter for one more second? Her plan would change Marcie's life for the better, too. She would have no more of Morris' oppression, no more of his absurd ideas about men and women. As for her own father, she would decide later what to do. Right now, a protection surrounded Lillian. She gave the buggy a sharp push away from the hubbub behind her, and limped toward the train.

On the platform, just before the porter lifted the buggy up the narrow stairs, a gust of wind blew a corner of the cloth cover back off the birdcage in front of Lillian. Inside, a crested white bird huddled down against the raw wind as its cage was handed up and onto the train. Next the buggy went up.

With the dignity of a grieving grandmother, Lillian handed her bag to the porter, took hold of his outstretched hand and pulled herself up the first step.

Acknowledgements

My true inspiration for this book came from the lives of my grandmothers. I have deep convictions against gender inequality in the world and about the struggles that women and all oppressed people face, and wanted to write a story that not only women could relate to, but also anyone who has struggled out of oppression to make a better life for themselves.

I owe a debt of gratitude to the women writers who have come before me to champion gender equality and make women's voices heard. They have inspired me to bring forth Lillian's story.

For Alexs Pate, my amazing teacher, mentor and friend; I can only say a thank you as big as the universe (and even *that's* not big enough). What serendipitous luck for us that we had a chance to work together and believe in each other.

For my daughter, Robin Simon, and my sons, Joe Price, Jacob Duscha, Charley Umbarger and Louis Umbarger; you have kept me tethered to life with love. Thank you.

For Paul, my husband – who is intelligent, generous, patient and kind, and who has given me the stability of love and the luxury of space so that I could endeavor to write a novel – I propose one long, ardent, continuous thank you. It is only because of your ceaseless and superlative work and support that this book is made real. I am so lucky to be with you.

A long time ago, my friend, Mark Flanders, suggested that there might be a novel waiting in my head. He was right, but I never could have written it without the help and loving support of many people, including the following, to whom I am especially grateful: Ingrid Liepins, Linda Cullen, Dr. SooJin Pate, Sarah Montes, Kay Prestgard, Joan Ellison and Mark Flanders, Sarah McNee, Marianne McNee, Ann Heltemes, Janet Collins, Mary Corddry, Art Fischbeck (Mason City historian), Sara Umbarger, Lloyd Umbarger, Friday Night Dinner Club, Sue Bickmore, Jeff Milligan-Toffler, Sarah Milligan-Toffler, Karen Lloyd, Dave Lloyd, Blue Daddies, Ellen Walsh, Nancy Tuminelly, Maureen Higgins, Dr. Richard Mayfield, Dr. Jean Montes, Marina Liadova, Anne Van Fleet, Dr. Jonathan May, Prue Morrison, Joe Sedarski, John Powers, Jim Umbarger, Annie Duerksen, Cheryl Tristam, Pierre Tristam, Sadie Tristam, Laura Lynn, Katina Taylor, Emily Graham, Wes Graham, Janine Newfield, Gabi Hänni, Rolf Hänni, Marianne Lerbs, and all of my students – every one.

About the Author

Coming To is Caren Umbarger's first novel. She earned her BA in violin performance from Hamline University and has been a professional musician and string teacher for thirty years. Caren grew up in Mason City, Iowa; taught, performed and conducted in Minneapolis for three decades; and is now the artistic director of a Florida youth orchestra program. She and her husband Paul, also a musician and artist, have five grown children. They live in St. Augustine with their two cats.

18320142R00140

Made in the USA
Charleston, SC
28 March 2013